"I think I knew all along that you would be the one to make  **control," Amarillo said. "That's why I s**

"Me?" Angelic

His gaze flick   of you. Being wit   of what I am. Fo   my feelings for you   on- scious I had them. But now   you, made love to you, I'm not sure I can find that kind of control again."

"Do you want to?"

"Yes."

She felt a stab of pain at his answer.

"And no, I don't want to. Now that I've had a taste of life with you, I'm not sure I can live without you."

She was overwhelmed. What would happen next was up to her.

Amarillo's long fingers framed her face. "Are you going to ask me to leave?"

"I don't have that kind of strength," she said, her voice hardly more than a breath.

His eyes darkened. "I couldn't have gone, even if you'd asked me to."

He put his arms around her, lifted her from the couch, and carried her to the bed. . . .

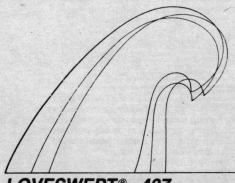

LOVESWEPT® • 437

Fayrene Preston
SwanSea Place:
The Jeopardy

BANTAM BOOKS
NEW YORK • TORONTO • LONDON • SYDNEY • AUCKLAND

THE JEOPARDY

A Bantam Book / November 1990

LOVESWEPT® and the wave device are registered
trademarks of Bantam Books, a division of
Bantam Doubleday Dell Publishing Group, Inc.
Registered in U.S. Patent
and Trademark Office and elsewhere.

If you would be interested in receiving protective vinyl
covers for your Loveswept books, please write to this
address for information:

Loveswept
Bantam Books
P. O. Box 985
Hicksville, NY 11802

ISBN 0-553-44068-3

Published simultaneously in the United States and Canada

Bantam Books are published by Bantam Books, a division
of Bantam Doubleday Dell Publishing Group, Inc. Its trademark, consisting of the words "Bantam Books" and the
portrayal of a rooster, is Registered in U.S. Patent and
Trademark Office and in other countries. Marca Regis-
trada. Bantam Books, 666 Fifth Avenue, New York, New
York 10103.

PRINTED IN THE UNITED STATES OF AMERICA

OPM   0 9 8 7 6 5 4 3 2 1

Preface

Bright golden sunshine and sweet breezes poured through the open French doors to fill the otherwise empty ballroom. Perfectly polished gold-edged mirrors caught the reflection of the ballroom's gleaming floors and the stately marble fireplace. Three huge crystal chandeliers glittered against the backdrop of a frescoed ceiling decorated with silver, gold, and mother-of-pearl swans and peacocks. The chandeliers were made up of layer after layer and row after row of petal-shaped crystal prisms, each as intricately cut and as sparkling as a diamond. The center chandelier, the largest, had been lowered by its pulley for cleaning and had not been returned to its high-ceilinged aerie.

At the end of the long room, a big door slowly opened and a little girl, her face alive with curiosity, intelligence, and spirit, peeked around it. And what she saw in the big, empty room made her golden eyes widen with delight.

The long mirrors reflected her image as she skipped toward the middle of the room. Why, she wondered, was such a splendid place empty? It was so bright and beautiful and warm. It had pictures of animals on the ceiling and mirrors on its walls. There was so much to do and see. What should she do first?

She stopped and glanced in a mirror. She definitely looked like a princess, she decided. Her white dress with its lace ruffles and petticoats was new, and she hadn't put one single run in her silk stockings, nor was there a single scuff mark on her white leather shoes. Even her satin hair ribbon was still in place. Nanny would be so pleased, she thought happily, and curtsied to herself. She giggled at her reflection and heard the faint echo of her giggle come back to her. How wonderful! She spread out her arms and twirled around and around until she was so dizzy she fell right on her bottom.

Laughing, she shook her head to clear it, then picked herself up and walked to the center chandelier. The just-washed crystals glinted and sparkled in the afternoon sunlight. She poked at one of the crystals, and colors shot out from its multifaceted prism to make a rainbow on her white dress. She poked at it again, harder this time, and the colored rainbow shimmered over her dress and onto the floor. Enchanted by her discovery, she circled the chandelier, running her fingers along the crystal petals. The movement created sweet, bell-like music that sounded like a choir of angels, she decided, while hundreds of rainbows danced and flashed over the floor and over her. It was all so exciting and so much fun.

"Arabella Linden, what are you doing?" a stern voice asked.

She squealed with pleasure at the sight of the tall, handsome man and ran to him, her arms outspread. "Papa! I'm so glad you're here. Isn't this a wondrous room?"

He scooped her into his arms and hugged her to him. She was all lace and satin and scuffed knees, his little Bella. "What do you have to say for yourself, young lady? I left you in the kitchen with the cook to have tea while I discussed business with Mr. Edward Deverell. I expected you to stay there until I came to get you."

"Mr. Deverell's eyes don't smile like yours do, Papa. Why is that?"

"Never mind about Mr. Deverell. I'm waiting for an explanation."

A practiced coquette with her father, she smoothed her finger back and forth over his starched collar. "I finished tea, and when Cook went out back to her garden, I decided to explore."

Her radiant smile could melt an iceberg, he thought with secret pride. "That was a very rude thing to do, Arabella. When Cook came back and found you gone, she became quite alarmed. We decided to organize a search party, and I volunteered to take the second floor."

"And you found me," she said brightly. "Clever Papa."

His mouth twitched with humor, but he did his best to keep his tone severe. "Your mother says I spoil you, and I'm beginning to think she's right. I brought you along with me this afternoon to give you a special treat, but you are going to make me regret it."

Her small face crumpled with dejection. "I'm sorry, Papa, but this is such a splendid house, I couldn't resist. I didn't mean to be gone long."

A look of puzzlement crossed his face. "Weren't you frightened being all alone up here? The halls are dark and most of the rooms are shut off."

She reached out a small hand and patted his cheek comfortingly. "There's nothing to be frightened of here at SwanSea."

He shook his head, not really understanding his small daughter. "Cook told me the only reason this room is open is because the maids were cleaning here. They'll be closing it up again within the hour."

She gave a small cry of distress. "But why? The room is special. It has rainbows in it."

He sighed. "Bella, Bella, what am I going to do with you? Well, never mind. I've found you, that's what's important for now." He set her on her feet, but kept her hand in his. "Let's go tell everyone you weren't lost after all. You had simply found a room with rainbows in it and were playing." He chuckled. "I can't wait to see Edward Deverell's face when I tell him that."

At the door she held back and looked over her shoulder. The room appeared golden in the afternoon sunlight. She smiled and lifted her small hand. "Good-bye," she whispered. "I'll try to come back one day."

Her father tugged on her hand. "Come on, Arabella."

She giggled and then she was gone. But the happy, warm feeling of her laughter remained . . . Even after the room was closed up again.

One

Angelica DiFrenza brushed a pink satin negligee set off the arm of her office chair, shoved the last piece of a Hershey bar into her mouth, and thoughtfully viewed her desk. Where was that printout of last week's sales figures? It had to be here . . . somewhere.

She seized a wine-colored high-heeled shoe that had been serving as a paperweight and tossed it over her shoulder; it hit the wall behind her with a soft thud, then bounced to the floor. An elegant crocodile bag suffered a similar fate as she chucked it across the room toward a mound of purses that was next to an open portfolio of dress sketches.

As she paused to take a swig of diet soda, her attention was caught by a short section of a rope of faux pearls sticking out from beneath a stack of orders. She freed the necklace and slung it over the corner of the chair's high back. Next she switched a basket of perfume samples from atop one pile of fabric samples to another, then shoved a box of shimmering beads to the edge of the desk. The action sent a pile of silk scarves fluttering from the desk to the floor.

And still there was no sign of the sales figures.

"Where is that damned printout?" she said, her words mumbled because of the chocolate in her mouth. "I saw it just a minute ago."

"Are you sure?"

Her head came up, and her eyes widened with surprise. Amarillo Smith lounged in her office doorway. For a moment her heart felt as if it had ceased to function. "Oh, Lord, has something happened to Nico and Caitlin?"

Immediately he pushed away from the doorjamb and advanced into the office. "No," he said quickly, his hard face and golden eyes somehow very reassuring, "there's nothing wrong. They're fine."

With a hand over her heart and a sigh of relief, she slumped against the back of her chair. "For a second—"

"Nico called me from Athens last night after he talked with you, and I'm sure he told me the same thing he told you. They're having a great time. I'm sorry if I frightened you."

She nodded, reflecting that he had caused her to feel many emotions over the years, but, with this one exception, he had never frightened her. Beneath her hand, her heart was pounding at an alarming rate.

She eyed him warily. He was her brother Nico's best friend and business partner in a private investigation firm. When he had first come to

Boston, he had joined forces with Nico to work with the police department. She had been a romantic sixteen, and he had been twenty-five and, to her, maddeningly attractive. Back then he had reminded her of a mountain lion, with his sandy hair, tawny gold eyes, and lean muscular body.

As she had grown older, she had become more and more uncomfortable in his presence. Her skin seemed to grow more sensitive whenever he was near, more susceptible to heat, cold, and nerves. And now at age twenty-seven, she recognized the raw, primitive sexuality he possessed as the potent weapon it was. He was a man who could affect her as no other. Acting with caution whenever he was near had become second nature to her.

"I don't know how you can locate anything in here. It looks more like a female version of Aladdin's cave than the office of a vice president of merchandising for Boston's most exclusive department store."

His normal speaking voice had always sounded to her like a low, seductive, sexy blend of a purr and a growl. Unerringly it found nerves hidden deep inside her.

With a quick gulp, she swallowed the last of the chocolate and surged to her feet. The faux pearls slid off the back of the chair to form an incandescent coil on the floor. "It's jet lag."

"I'm sure you're right."

She saw no expression on his rugged face, but she could feel the power of his gaze on her. It seemed to linger a second too long on her breasts where the lace of her slip showed like a faint pattern through her white silk blouse. After that it followed the length of the long gold chains that circled her neck and fell over her breasts to her waist. Finally it traced the lines of her short violet leather skirt as it gloved the curve of her hips and the firmness of her thighs.

She felt touched all over.

Yet surely her imagination was working overtime. He had long ago made it clear, first by aloofness, then by his indifference, that he wasn't interested in her, and it was ridiculous to let him throw her so off balance.

She willed a return of her composure. "I meant that usually I know exactly where everything is. Believe it or not, there's organization in my disorganization."

"I believe you," he said in his drawling purr. "Nico brags about you all the time. It's obvious to everyone who knows you that you've worked hard to achieve your position here."

"It is?" she asked, stunned, not because of what had been said but because of who had said it. She was sure Amarillo didn't think of her often enough to have *any* opinion whatsoever about her. "I'm glad to hear it. I've never wanted anyone to be able to say that my position was given to me because my great-grandmother founded the store and my father is the current head."

"Do you really care what people think?"

"I guess it depends on who the person is," she said slowly, then realized she was staring too hard at him. "At any rate, I just returned from

California yesterday, and I'm still a little out of sync."

"Too many hours in the sky can do that to you."

So could being too near him, she thought, and decided to cut through the small talk. "What are you doing here, Amarillo?"

A line deepened in the center of his brow. He didn't like her question, she thought, but it was natural for her to ask. After all, he had never, ever sought her out. She had last seen him about a month before at a dinner party given by Caitlin and Nico. He had been with a blonde named Terri. She had been with Bob Worthing, an old friend from college. And, as usual, whenever she and Amarillo happened to be at the same function, he had treated her with a polite and definitely distant friendliness.

But now he was here in her office, and she knew he rarely did anything without a purpose. Since he obviously didn't intend to answer her question until he was ready, she indicated a George III open armchair in front of her desk. "Would you like to sit down? Those dresses—just move them anywhere."

Amarillo scooped up an armful of gaily patterned dresses, deposited them on a couch, then brought his long-framed body down into the chair. "Your trip to California," he said quietly after he was settled. "It was simply out and back, right?"

"Yes. I pushed three days' worth of meetings into one and flew home." She paused. "How did you know it was a turnaround trip?"

"Nico. He mentioned it last night when he called."

She nodded. "Where did he say they were going next? I can't remember."

"They're going to Rome. And he mentioned that you didn't seem quite with it when you talked."

All at once she understood, and a smile touched her lips. "Ah, okay, now I know what you're doing here. My big brother asked you to drop by and check up on me."

"If I was in the neighborhood . . ."

She arched her delicate brow, her skepticism clear. "Uh-huh. And DiFrenza's was in your neighborhood?"

"I needed a tie."

She had no idea where he shopped, but she knew it wasn't DiFrenza's. His style was strictly western, and DiFrenza's was Boston traditional along with international high fashion. "I don't see a package."

"I didn't find anything I liked."

"I apologize. I'll have to have a talk with my buyer of men's wear."

"Instead of doing that, why don't you tell me what's wrong?"

His voice was soft, low-pitched. She wondered why she felt he had given her an order.

"There's nothing wrong."

His gaze didn't waver from her. She sighed. "Look, I don't know what time it was in Athens when Nico called, but here in Boston it was midnight and I was almost asleep."

"Since when have you ever gone to bed before midnight?"

"How do you know what time I go to bed?"

A casual shrug sent the golden-brown material of his western-cut jacket shifting across his broad shoulders. "It's a guess. Your social life seems too active for you to be getting much rest."

If she didn't know better, she would think he had been keeping track of her. It was an interesting thought, but one in which she put absolutely no credence. "Well, you're right. I don't often get to bed before midnight. But in this case, the trip had left me tired and with a bad case of jet lag. And when Nico called, he got a disoriented conversation from someone who badly needed sleep. Simple as that."

"Uh-huh. And *did* you get any sleep last night?"

Something darted across her mind and then was gone. Troubled, she rubbed at her forehead. She'd had a dream last night—a bad dream—but this morning she hadn't been able to remember what it had been about. "Yes, I slept. Some."

"Must have been one hell of a trip."

He rose and was around the desk before she had time to prepare herself. His nearness was as exciting as it seemed dangerous.

He picked up the wastebasket and fished out four candy wrappers. "Breakfast and lunch?"

"Candy is an excellent source of energy."

"So is a balanced meal and a good night's rest." He set the wastebasket down and shoved his hands into his pockets.

The brooding intensity of his gaze had her spine tingling. Amarillo was not a womanizer, she knew, but Caitlin had once told her that women used the word *fatal* when speaking of him. Angelica had long understood how a woman could lose herself and her heart to him. Yet from what she had heard and seen, he never lost anything but interest where a woman was concerned.

"Come have lunch with me."

His astonishing request yanked her from her contemplation. She was sure few of his invitations were turned down. If the circumstances were right, she might . . . *No*. Besides, these definitely weren't the right circumstances. He was here only because he was doing a favor for Nico, and she loathed the idea of being Amarillo's charity case.

"I'm sorry, but I can't." She waved a hand toward her desk. "I have too much work to do here, plus the charity ball at SwanSea is just around the corner. Since Caitlin is out of the country, I'm chairing the event."

As she spoke, Amarillo studied her carefully. Her dark brown hair shone with health and vibrancy, her skin glowed with its usual luminosity, her brown eyes still held that incredible velvet texture that could melt a man at fifty paces. She appeared perfectly normal. Nico must have reached her at a bad time, he concluded. Other than a mild case of exhaustion, Amarillo couldn't detect anything that might be bothering her.

Unlike he—who was bothered just by looking at her.

"I read the writeup in the paper last week about the ball and your part in it. Nice picture, by the way."

She grimaced. She did not enjoy her picture appearing in the papers, though she realized she differed from most people in that respect. "Thanks. Anyway, as soon as I can get things under control here, I'll be driving up to SwanSea."

Why did he feel so disappointed that there was nothing wrong? Amarillo wondered, glancing restlessly around the office. The clutter made a perfect setting for her. Silks and satins. High-heeled shoes and pearls. Warm, feminine, mind-destroyingly sexy. "How long do you think it will take to wind things up?"

"Not long now that I'm back. I've nearly cleared my desk as it is."

"You have a unique way of working."

She shrugged, determined not to be swayed by the hint of humor she heard threading through his tone. Nothing changed the fact that he was there as a favor to Nico. "I suppose I do, but the main thing is I get results. I'm really sorry, Amarillo. Lunch is out of the question."

"No problem. We'll have dinner."

Despite her intention to keep this sudden new attention of his in perspective, a spurt of excitement shot into her bloodstream. He wasn't going to let the matter drop. She drew a deep breath and tried again. "It's very nice of you to come check on me for Nico, but you don't have to ask me out. As you can see for yourself, I'm fine."

"I'm glad to hear it, but I'm still asking." He had no idea why he was being so persistent, he reflected with annoyance. He had meant only to drop by, stay a minute or two, then leave. Last night when Nico had called him, he had wanted to go to her immediately. The urge had puzzled him. Nico hadn't sounded alarmed, just mildly concerned. Still, he reasoned, Nico trusted him to take care of everything while he and Caitlin were gone, and if that included keeping an eye on Nico's kid sister, so be it. "If you come, I promise you chocolate."

She laughed. "You sound like you're bribing me."

He didn't even smile, because that was exactly what he was doing. Except, he knew very well she was no longer a young girl to be tempted by a treat. "Come directly from work to my place." He drew a pad and pen from his jacket, scribbled his address on it, then tore the top sheet from the pad and handed it to her. "Seven-thirty all right?"

She gazed at the piece of paper in her hand. She had always been curious about Amarillo, his private life, where and how he lived, what he did in his spare time. But— "Wouldn't it be easier to call Nico and tell him he overreacted, that I'm all right, simply overworked?"

"I'll do that too."

She shook her head, confused. "I don't understand why you feel you need to take me to dinner."

His lips twisted into a wry grin. "Maybe, Angelica, I don't want to eat alone."

"But I'm sure there's someone, a woman, you would enjoy being with—"

"There is. You."

She gazed up at him, trying to decide what to do. All her instincts told her to remain firm. But how did she say no to this man? His jawline looked as if it had been sandblasted from granite;

the golden color of his eyes drew, the secrets they seemed to guard enticed.

"Do you already have plans?" he asked. "Did you plan to eat at all?"

"Of course. Amarillo—"

"Give me a reason why not."

"A reason?"

"Why not, Angelica?" he said, repeating the question. "Why not go to dinner with me?"

The shape and force of the words stirred the air around her. The power of the man overwhelmed her.

She wanted badly to go. One minute she was fighting the urge. The next she gave up with a light laugh. "I guess you're right. Why not?"

"Good," he said softly. "I'll see you at seven-thirty." He bent and drew a computer printout from the wastebasket. "These may be the sales figures you were looking for. Try not to work too hard."

After he had gone, she gazed down at the sheet he had handed her. They were exactly what she had been looking for.

The phone rang. With a soft smile on her face, she walked to her desk to answer it. "Angelica DiFrenza."

"Be a good girl and mind me."

She went motionless at the high-pitched, muffled voice. "Who is this?"

"Be a good girl and stay home, where you belong."

She slammed the receiver into its cradle.

Judith, her secretary, popped her head into the

office. "Hi, I'm back from lunch. Is everything all right? That was a rather loud hangup."

She ran her hand around the back of her neck and eyed the phone with the same distaste she would a snake. "Oh, it's nothing. Some crank, that's all. He called me last night too. I think he even said pretty much the same thing."

And Nico had called immediately afterward, she remembered. Without realizing it, she must have sounded disturbed, and he had picked up on it.

"I don't like the sound of a crank call. Is there someone we can notify? Make sure it doesn't happen again?"

She shook her head. "No, no. It's no big deal. It's happened to me a time or two before. This guy will get tired of calling me soon. The others did."

Two

Angelica slid out of her car, locked its door, then paused to survey her surroundings. The address Amarillo had given her was actually a large riverfront warehouse. Her interest heightened. And her nerves worsened.

She smoothed her hands down her slender leather skirt, straightened the matching jacket, and reflected with uncertainty that perhaps she should have changed. She often went on dates right from work, but then, this definitely was not a date—though she wasn't entirely certain what it was.

Amarillo viewed this night as fulfilling some sort of commitment to Nico. In that light, perhaps she should simply look on this evening as a dinner with her brother's best friend. A *casual* evening. Yeah, sure.

The rain that had fallen all afternoon had stopped, leaving the narrow blacktopped street slick, mirrored, and surrealistic. Angelica started toward the warehouse. Large windows lined its long side, but the only light she could see was a small yellow bulb over a door. She knocked several times, but there was no answer. Could she be at the wrong place?

Gingerly she stepped into the flower bed, worked her way to a window, and peered in. Large indistinct shapes loomed in the darkness. Startled, she jerked away. She *had* to be at the wrong place. She returned to the light and pulled the paper Amarillo had given her from her pocket.

"Hey, *you!*"

She spun and saw an elderly woman approaching. The woman was dressed in tan pants, an oversize red flannel shirt, and a brown felt hat pulled down tightly on her head.

"Is there something I can help you with?" the woman asked in a gruff voice. A long, thin cigarette dangled from her mouth, and she carried a brown paper bag filled with groceries.

Angelica held out a slip of paper. "I'm looking for the address written here."

The woman scanned it, then looked back at Angelica. "So you've come to see Rill, have you?"

"You know Amarillo?"

"Sure. He's my landlord." She took a long draw from her cigarette, then nodded toward her grocery bag. "I had to go get some things to eat. Couldn't stand his nagging anymore. He's got a thing about regular meals. My own children couldn't care less what I eat. Fat chance they're going to get *my* money. They make pompous asses a fun crowd to hang around with."

Angelica absorbed this. "Uh, does Amarillo lives here?"

"His place is in the back of the building." The woman pointed toward the water. "My studio is here in front, facing town. But I don't care what's outside my window as long as I've got the space I need on the inside."

Angelica thought of the huge shapes she had seen through the window. "Why is that?"

"I work here." She put down her bag and held out her hand. "I'm Metta."

Angelica took her hand as the name tripped something in her mind, but she couldn't grasp what it was. Her memory was really slipping lately, she reflected ruefully. She hadn't been able to recall last night's dream either, but then, she reassured herself, most people didn't remember their dreams. "I'm Angelica DiFrenza."

The woman's face magically cleared. "You're Nico's sister! Well, what do you know. And you're every bit as pretty as he said."

"Thank you. You've very kind."

Metta's laugh sounded like a bark. "That's certainly a new and novel opinion. Feel free to come around more."

"She doesn't give an invitation like that often," Amarillo said to Angelica, coming up behind her. "In fact, almost never."

Angelica turned. In the strange yellow light, his face seemed all angles and shadows, and his golden eyes appeared to glow.

"I was wondering what was keeping you," he said softly, scrutinizing her every bit as closely as she was him.

She definitely should have changed, she thought. "I wasn't sure I was at the right place. Metta saw me and—"

"You don't have to say any more," he said dryly. "I get the picture. Once Metta starts talking, it's hard to get away."

Scowling, Metta bent to pick up her groceries, but Amarillo beat her to the package, lifted it, and handed it to her. "I don't know why I put up with you, Amarillo Smith. You're lousy as a landlord. You've never once asked me for rent."

He shrugged. "I keep forgetting."

"Well, it's a damned nuisance. Every month I have to track you down to give you the money."

"I've told you not to worry about it."

Metta sent a glaring look at Angelica. "You can see the problem, can't you? The boy doesn't have a bit of business sense. And what's more, if I didn't water the flowers, they would die as sure as you're standing there."

"Who planted them?" Amarillo asked, countering her.

"So what if I did plant them? You look at them, don't you?"

As far as Angelica could tell, Amarillo was totally unfazed by Metta's fussing. In fact, both he and his tenant seemed to be enjoying themselves . . . immensely.

"Ummph. I've wasted enough time talking to you. I've got work to do." She inserted the key in her door, then paused to look over her shoulder. "By the way, Rill. I think you've finally got yourself a winner."

"She's Nico's sister."

"So?"

"It was nice meeting you, Metta," Angelica said to fill the silence that ensued, but Metta had already gone into her studio and shut the door firmly behind her.

"Interesting lady," she murmured.

"She's a complete eccentric and a great friend." He took her arm and guided her away from the warehouse. "She's also the finest metal sculptor in the New England area."

"Really? There was something about her name that sounded familiar to me, but—"

"Metta is short for Mehetabel."

"That was *Mehetabel*? Everyone's heard of her work. I'm sorry to say, though, I don't think I've ever seen any other than in art publications."

"I have several pieces by her," he said, "but I'm displaying only one at the moment."

"I'd like to see it."

He hesitated, and she sensed that he was about to turn her down.

But in the next moment he shrugged. "We can come back to my place after we've had dinner if you like."

"I would." They were walking diagonally across the street now. "Where are we going?"

"Le Marèe Cramoisi."

She gasped with delight. "I've been there, and it's wonderful!"

He felt his pulse quicken as her lovely features became suddenly animated. She took his breath away. She always did, those times when he made the mistake of paying too much attention to her or of looking too long at her.

"I didn't realize Le Marèe Cramoisi was walking distance from your place," she said, continuing. "It's a very exclusive restaurant, and reservations are almost impossible to get."

"That's what I hear." He steered her into an alley. "Hungry?"

"Starved." She laughed and realized that her encounter with Metta had been so interesting, she had forgotten to be nervous with him. She hoped the feeling lasted. "What *is* this thing you have about feeding people? Metta said you nag her, too, about eating."

"She gets so involved with her work, she forgets to eat. It's not good for her." He smiled briefly. "I hadn't thought of it before, but I don't think it's really about *feeding* people. It's more to do with seeing a situation that needs to be taken care of and taking care of it."

Her high-heeled shoes clicked on the pavement of the narrow alley. "Is that what I am? A situation?"

His tawny gold eyes caught the light from a nearby doorway, causing them to glint strangely. "No. You're Angelica."

His flat, emotionless tone left her disconcerted, but she didn't have time to pursue it further, because he guided her toward the light, opened the door, and ushered her into a stainless-steel and white-tile kitchen where confusion seemed to reign supreme.

She blinked as a melody of rich scents and a cacophony of sounds assaulted her. "I thought we were going to Le Marèe Cramoisi."

"We're here."

"Rill! 'Bout damned time you got here." A big man dressed all in white and built on the order of a large, thick-trunked tree came striding toward them. "How can I plan a tour de force if I don't know when you'll get here?" he roared in a heavy Alabama accent.

And hearing the accent, Angelica understood why the restaurant was named Le Marèe Cramoisi, The Crimson Tide.

"Hell's bells, Rill, you have no idea what goes into creating a perfect sauce."

Amarillo grinned. "Are you saying you can't handle it?"

"Of *course* I'm not saying that, you fool!"

Amarillo turned to her. "Angelica, meet Beauregard Hamilton, the owner and chef of this fine establishment and our host for this evening."

"Call me Beau." He took her hand and exuberantly pumped it. "Angelica, prepare yourself for a feast. Tonight you will experience culinary delights you never imagined."

She found his enthusiasm contagious. "I'm sure I will, and I can't wait."

"That's what I like to hear! Take a seat and we'll get you fed." He hurried away and disappeared back into the confusion.

"Take a seat?" She glanced at Amarillo for guidance.

He pointed toward several high metal stools in front of a stainless steel counter. When her expression turned to amazement, he grinned. "I always eat in the kitchen. I like the atmosphere better than out front. Less stuffy."

He'd rather eat in the kitchen, she thought, yet

she had seen him at sophisticated social gatherings perfectly at ease and elegant in a tuxedo. And he shared a warehouse with a prickly sculptress, provided her with an obvious sanctuary, made sure she ate, and took rent from her only because she insisted.

After all this time she was beginning to learn some things about Amarillo. And she was enjoying herself immensely.

At the counter she hitched her tight skirt halfway up her thighs and began to lever herself onto the stool. He automatically reached out to help her, grasping her waist to give her a needed boost. She felt a flash of warmth in her stomach. If being with Amarillo in even the most casual of ways could bring this kind of excitement and heat, Angelica reflected, what would it be like to be his lover? Perhaps it was better, safer, not to know the answer to that question.

She slipped out of her jacket and laid it and her purse on the counter beside her. The air on her right side heated as Amarillo came down on the next stool over. Self-conscious and nervous again, she said the first thing that came into her mind. "I'm afraid I didn't have time to change before I came."

"You look fine, as always." A muscle jerked in his cheek.

Angelica glanced at him, then away. He was irritated with her. *She* was irritated with herself. Why did *he* have to be the only person in the world with whom she became awkward and tongue-tied?

Food began to be served, a French version of

dim sum first. She tasted everything from lobster in wine sauce to delicate veal in cream sauce and chicken breast stuffed with mushrooms and Gruyère cheese. Complementing the entrees was a clear sherried beef bouillon with chives sprinkled on top, along with julienne carrots steamed with butter and tarragon, followed by bundles of green beans and straw mushrooms wrapped in strips of leeks.

And so it went, until finally Angelica put her hand across her stomach and groaned. "I'll never eat again."

"I say that every time I come here," Amarillo said, "but it never quite seems to work out that way."

Just at that moment Beau appeared, wheeling a cart that bore a huge chocolate confection. He presented it with a great flourish. "It is called Chocolate Angelica, in your honor, my dear, and will be introduced tonight in the restaurant for the first time."

Angelica cast a helpless glance at Amarillo.

He smiled. "I did promise you chocolate."

She'd seen him smile many times before, but rarely at her. She was captivated by the unexpected twinkle in his eye and the amused sensual curve of his lips.

"It looks superb," he said to Beau.

"It is superb!" the big man boomed. "Of course it is! It couldn't be anything else. *I* created it. Angelica, darlin', I will explain. What you have here is a chocolate gateau with chocolate mousse piped on top, surrounded by strawberries hand-dipped in both white and milk chocolate and drizzled with crushed raspberries."

Amarillo reached for a spoon, scooped up a portion, and fed it to her. It melted in her mouth. "It tastes as if it were made in heaven," she assured Beau, who had been watching her closely for a reaction.

"Naturally!" He smiled broadly and patted her on the back. "This one is yours. Eat. Enjoy. Be happy."

"Uh, Beau? I wonder if I could trouble you to wrap it up for me so that I can take it home and eat it later?" She saw Beau's face begin to darken and she hastened to add, "I'll eat it *all*. I *promise*."

"She'll have it for breakfast tomorrow," Amarillo said.

She couldn't help but grin at him. He had read her mind.

They left the restaurant in silence, Amarillo carrying the gateau in a white cake box. As they neared the warehouse, she could see lights burning in Metta's studio.

"Metta's working late."

"She enjoys working at night. Fewer people to bother her, she says."

"I gather she's not much of a people person."

"No, but she liked you."

They walked in the direction of the river, and soon they were at the warehouse and a door well hidden by shrubs. When he opened it, he stepped back to allow her to precede him. She hesitated and glanced up at him. Part of his face was concealed by darkness, but she had the sudden, strange feeling he would rather not have her in his home.

"What's the matter?" he asked softly.

"I don't know."

His lips quirked sardonically, as if he had read her mind, but with a wave of his hand he indicated she should enter.

She walked into a space of mammoth dimensions, and for a second she could only stare, amazed. Across the front of the building, two wide half-circle windows went from floor to ceiling and wall to wall. During the day the windows would offer a spectacular view of the river. As it was, she could see lights glinting in the dark water like fallen stars.

Her attention returned to the interior. The predominant colors of burgundy and hunter green created a dark, rich, intimate feeling in spite of the immense dimensions. The furniture was oversized and overstuffed. Tall bookcases served as dividers. Tapestries and prayer rugs hung alone, suspended from the tall ceiling and from the back of the dividers. Plants and room-size trees abounded. An ebony staircase led up to a large second floor loft—no doubt the bedroom area, she thought. And in a corner there was a huge bronze sculpture of a rearing horse, its mane flying.

"It's Metta's work," he said from behind her.

He moved so quietly, she hadn't known he was near. But now her skin reacted, and a quiver of warmth skimmed along her arms and up her legs. She swallowed against the sudden tightness of her throat. "I guessed that. And the Stetson hanging on one of the legs?"

"Mine."

"What does Metta have to say about your using her work as a hat rack?"

"She thinks it's a great idea that someone's finally found a practical purpose for it."

She laced her fingers together. "Your home is terrific. I really like it. It's . . . unexpected, very unusual."

His lips moved in a suggestion of a smile. "What did you expect? Ranch house furniture and an open campfire?"

"Something like that, I guess. Pretty stereotypical thinking, huh? Actually, this place is very much like you."

"Why is that?"

She knew there was a touch of the provocative in her answer, but she decided not to let that stop her. "Because I have a feeling no matter how much I explored, I would never see everything."

He stilled, and she waited for his reaction. Silence surrounded her, but her senses picked up danger.

When he finally spoke, though, all he said was, "Would you like something to drink? Coffee, brandy, something else . . . ?"

"Coffee will be fine."

His expression moody, he lightly touched a finger to her cheek. "Explore, Angelica."

He disappeared behind a divider, and she was left to deal with the wash of heat sweeping through her. For a moment she stayed where she was, feeling and absorbing the sensation. But his invitation was a lure she couldn't resist for long.

The bookcases held a wide assortment of books—leather-bound, hardcover, paperback. The latest Stephen King novel stood beside the complete works of Shakespeare. A row of scientific books marched above a row of Louis L'Amour westerns.

She continued around the room and found a Regency mahogany Pembroke worktable that held a large baccarat bowl filled with arrowheads. Further on, an exquisitely tooled, silver-trimmed saddle was displayed beneath a French Impressionist painting.

She noticed a red button, pushed it, and jumped with surprise when an electric train chugged out from under a table, smoke billowing from its smokestack. Its track had been arranged in areas where people wouldn't normally walk, and the little train cheerfully wound under and around the furniture and traveled over fine Oriental rugs and gleaming hardwood floors.

Obviously Amarillo Smith was a man who did things in a different way, and, it took not a second for her to realize, she loved his way of doing things. The revelation shook her.

"Here it is," he said, returning with two cups of steaming coffee and handing her one.

"Thank you." She chose to sit on the nearest couch. He dropped down onto the same couch not too far from her.

She took a sip of the coffee. The hot black liquid fortified her. Then it hit her. He hadn't asked if she took cream or sugar. He had known she didn't. No, she immediately corrected herself. He must have guessed.

She was surrounded by contradictions and puzzles. A French Impressionist painting and a show saddle. A crystal bowl and a collection of arrowheads. An electric train and Oriental carpets. And heading the list of contradictions and puzzles was Amarillo.

She turned to him. "You grew up in West Texas, didn't you?"

"That's right."

"I've never been there. I've seen pictures of it, though."

"No photograph could begin to capture what it's like."

There was a tone akin to reverence in his deep voice. Her better judgment told her she couldn't afford to be any more intrigued with him than she already was, but her curiosity was strong. "Then tell me."

"Telling is easy. It's miles of nothing but wind and barbed wire, sand and dust, mesquite and coyotes. But you can't understand its immensity or its spirit unless you go there and see for yourself."

"You sound as if you really love it."

"I do. West Texas is cruel and elemental, but it also has a very special kind of beauty."

And using all those elements, it had formed a man like Amarillo, she thought.

She wanted to ask why he had left, but she already knew at least part of the story, enough to know she shouldn't ask more. Nico had once told her that Amarillo had married a girl he had met in college. A year later his wife had been killed in a tragic accident, and he had moved to Boston, where her elderly parents lived, to be near them and care for them. She had heard that they had both died within the last two years.

"I go back as often as I can," he said continuing. "I have business interests there."

She hadn't known, but then, there was no reason she should. She usually made an effort to stay away from him. That's why she was amazed when she heard herself saying, "You're coming to the ball, aren't you? I'm counting on you to buy a table. It's for the Children's Fund."

His lids dropped to half veil his eyes. "How about I just give you the money?"

"You're not coming?" She set her coffee aside; he did the same.

"With Nico away, I don't feel I should leave things unattended here. We have a number of ongoing cases at the moment. . . ."

"I also happen to know that you have a large staff of very competent people."

"I guess I'm arrogant enough to think that things won't be done properly unless I'm at the office to oversee them."

He was giving her a polite, socially acceptable excuse, she reflected. She should accept it. He obviously did not want to be at SwanSea at the same time she was, at least not without the buffer of Caitlin and Nico. She was relieved, she told herself. With a glance at her watch, she stood. "It's midnight. It's time I was going."

He didn't argue with her. "I'll walk you to your car."

* * *

A fog had moved in since they had been inside. It swirled around them in feathery patterns, parting as they moved through it, then closing behind them again. Water lapped, a boat moved up the river, a foghorn sounded in the distance.

To Angelica, the night had an otherworldly feel about it, but then again, the whole evening had been out of the ordinary for her.

She opened the car door. Amarillo leaned in, put the cake box in the seat next to hers, then straightened.

"Thank you for this evening," she said. "I had a lovely time."

He nodded without expression.

"Give me a good report when you talk to Nico."

"I will."

He was waiting for her to get in the car and drive away, but she couldn't quite make herself leave him yet. She knew the next time she saw him, they would be surrounded by other people. He would be with someone else, as she would. The two of them would probably never again be alone together in just this way, wrapped in night and fog.

On impulse, she stood on tiptoe and pressed a kiss to his cheek.

The touch of her lips on his skin was a shock to his entire system. His hand came out to steady her, but when she was standing again, he couldn't seem to release his grip on her arm. Even through the leather jacket he could feel how soft she was. And the way she smelled . . . Her scent whispered around him, leaving in its trail a sensual impression of satin and velvet.

Earlier he had watched unobserved as she had wandered around his home, looking at and touching objects and furnishings he had collected over the years, leaving prints and impressions of herself on his things that he doubted could ever be wiped away. She was insidious; she was all things female. He wanted to sink into the scented femininity of her and soak himself.

With a growl of anger and despair he drew her against him and brought his mouth down on hers. And immediately his tongue found hers. He had never thought he would kiss her, yet, surprisingly, he already knew the delectable taste of her and even the irresistible rose-petal texture of her skin.

He slid his hand beneath her jacket and up her back. He felt silk. And fire, low in his stomach. The silk didn't take him unaware. The fire did. It was instant and all-consuming. How could that be? What was the explanation? It bothered him that he didn't know. He didn't like things that bothered him.

Abruptly he wrenched his mouth away, but the sight of her, fresh from being kissed by him, nearly undid him. Her skin was flushed with desire, her lips were parted and moist, ready for more of his kisses. He gritted his teeth until his jaw hurt. "We need to stop, Angelica."

"Do we?"

Her question carried a soft, bewildered innocence that played havoc with his senses. He could have her. . . .

"Yes, dammit, we do." With a barely suppressed violence he shoved the car door closed, pushed her back to it, then brought himself down on her, increasing the pressure against her until every curve of her body was impressed into him. He looked down at her for a second longer, his eyes hard and glittery. "Yes," he said again, this time with a thick whisper. "We do." And he took her mouth with his.

She shouldn't be giving in this easily, she reflected hazily, then wondered why she thought she should resist. Her mind was having a hard time catching up to the idea of this sudden frantic need she felt for him, but the truth was she wanted him with a desperation that was growing by the second. She burrowed her fingers through his hair and gave herself up to him.

A fever raged in his blood and in his head. He pulled at her blouse until it was loose from the waistband, then quickly unbuttoned her blouse. "I've wanted to do this forever," he muttered. "Forever." Impatiently he shoved her slip and bra straps off her shoulder, then delved beneath the lace to what he sought.

Her skin burned as his hand moved over her, caressing and kneading until the pleasure threatened her reason. Her breasts swelled and throbbed, and she began to squirm, trying to get closer to him. There was an aching in her that cried out for relief. Then his fingers found the nipple, and the pleasure took on an edge that brought her close to madness. Needs, wants, desires joined, grew, until she was lost in the passion, in the fog, in him.

Frustrated by the restriction of her clothes, desperate to have her, he cupped her hips and lifted her, sliding her up the car until he could bend his head and draw the tightly beaded nipple he had been tormenting into his mouth. And as soon as he did, a hard shudder raced through him. From having nothing of her to being on his way to having everything of her within the space of a few seconds was almost too much for him. Glorious and powerful sensations were overwhelming him. He had feared it would be like this.

He tightened his hold on her and sucked strongly, pulling at the nipple. Her sweet, mindless moans and gasps entered his brain, inflaming and urging him on.

Suddenly another sound intruded, a metallic, grating sound, and everything in him tensed, then froze. Reality came rushing back. Metta was using her grinder, he realized. With a violent oath he wrenched away and lowered her until her feet touched the ground.

It was as if she had suddenly been deprived of oxygen. She felt dizzy, confused, bereft. "Amarillo?" she whispered. "What happened?"

"Damned good question." A scowl deepened the lines of his face. With jerky motions he reached out and straightened her clothes.

He started to say something, then stopped. He lifted his hand as if he would touch her, then let it drop. Abruptly he turned and walked away.

Angelica felt as if a steamroller had just driven over her. He had walked away from her!

Her eyes hurt as she stared into the fog, but it had swallowed him up without a trace. She was completely alone, as if he had never been there with her. But her body knew better. Beneath the silk blouse her skin still burned where his hands had touched and her breast still ached for the feel of his mouth once again.

Why had he left her? Her mind screamed out the question, but no answer came back to her.

She swatted at her suddenly damp face with the back of her hand and came to the conclusion that Amarillo had the right idea. It was time to leave.

Once more at home, standing by one of the huge windows, Amarillo gazed out at the night. Why in God's name had he done something as stupid as even getting *near* Angelica, much less kissing her? Years ago, with great deliberation, he had mentally pushed her out of the inner circle of his life. Over time he had watched as she had danced and laughed, fascinating first one young man and then another. He had been unmoved by the sight.

But then, suddenly, tonight he had closed the distance between them—and all it had taken was the feel of her lips on his cheek as she had given him a brotherly kiss good night. Something had snapped inside him. He had come undone.

His gut was tied in painful knots. He had to regain the distance between them, because if he didn't, he was very much afraid that the one kiss and all that had gone with it would just be the start. He picked up a pillow and hurled it across the room.

* * *

Angelica closed the door of her renovated brownstone behind her and collapsed back against it. She felt as if a storm had thundered through her world and turned everything upside down.

She closed her eyes and remembered. The fog. The river sounds. Amarillo's mouth on hers, on her breast. Her blood turned hot merely thinking about it. It was almost as if there'd been a part of her that had been waiting all these years for the moment when he would take her into his arms and make love to her. It was hard for her to believe, even harder for her to admit to herself, but it was true. And they had almost made love.

The intensity of what had happened between them jolted her to her very core. She wasn't a woman to forget everything and let herself go completely with a man, no matter *who* the man was.

But the scary thing was she had done just that. And the man had been Amarillo.

What was he thinking about her, feeling about her? *He* had been the one to break away. She had been willing to—

The phone rang, and her heart leapt into her throat. *Amarillo.*

She raced to the phone and answered breathlessly. "Hello?"

"I told you to be a good girl, but you're not minding."

She began to tremble. "W-what?"

"Good girls shouldn't go out. They should stay home and do as they're told."

The line went dead. Slowly she replaced the receiver in its cradle. Her hand went to her forehead and found it damp with perspiration.

Don't you dare let this get to you, she ordered herself. Everyone got the occasional crank call.

Then why did this one bother her so much?

She wrapped her arms around her waist and hugged herself tightly. She supposed it was natural to be a little upset. Any woman who lived alone would be.

But the call meant nothing. Nothing.

Three

"Good morning, Miss DiFrenza."

"Good morning, Miss DiFrenza."

Angelica smiled and murmured "good morning" in response to the cheerful choruses of greeting. It was a routine she went through each morning as she arrived at work and made her way to her office. The store her great-grandmother, Elena, had founded was in her blood, and she loved everything about it, always had, ever since she was a little girl and Elena had brought her to work with her. The symmetry and order reflected in the layout of display cases and clothes racks pleased her, the smells and textures of the different types of merchandise made her happy.

But today a disturbance rippled beneath the pleasant familiarity of her routine. She had dreamt in the night. When she had awakened, she had been left with only vaguely disquieting wisps of the dream. Why was it bothering her, she wondered. And why was she giving more than a moment's thought to the antics of her mind while she slept? Dreams never made sense anyway.

Which brought her to the subject that was truly worthy of disturbing her, she thought gloomily—what had happened between her and Amarillo the night before.

In her office Angelica sank into her chair and viewed the jumble on her desk. As usual, the open calendar containing her day's schedule sat square in the middle. Judith had an energetic first-grader who needed breakfast, wardrobe consultation, and a ride to school every morning. Consequently, she was unable to arrive at work the same time Angelica did. But each evening before she went home, she always positioned the calendar on the desk so that it was impossible to miss.

Uncharacteristically Angelica ignored the calendar and gazed instead at the phone. Would Amarillo be in his office yet? He had seemed so angry when he had stalked away. Why? What had happened? Had she done something wrong? Anything other than practically dissolve in his arms, that is?

Dammit. Her hand sent the calendar and a pile of fabric samples to the floor. She had to stop thinking like that! But how? *She* had been the one left to deal with feelings of acute embarrassment and humiliation. *He* had walked away.

"Miss DiFrenza? I wonder if I might have a word with you before you get too busy."

Angelica looked up to see William Breckinridge, the man who had headed DiFrenza's jewelry department for the past ten years, standing in her office doorway. The call to Amarillo would have to wait, she thought. Smothering her impatience and pasting a smile on her face, she said, "Come in, Mr. Breckinridge. Actually, you are on my list to see today."

"I hope it's about the charity ball. We do need to talk."

"Yes, we do. Won't you sit down?" She indicated a chair, reflecting that he was the only employee with whom she worked who waited for her to ask him to sit.

"I'll stand if you don't mind."

She sighed. "Not at all. Whatever is most comfortable for you." He was a man in his early fifties with silver hair and a formality that only could have been with him from birth. Fortunately there was no doubt that DiFrenza's customers enjoyed his rather stuffy, even superior manner. She supposed it gave a certain ceremony and importance to the matter of paying thousands for a necklace or a pair of earrings. Normally she was all for anything that helped sales, but this morning she found his attitude irritating.

"I suppose the ladies have been calling, asking about borrowing jewelry for the ball," she said. Elena DiFrenza had initiated a policy that the store's best customers could borrow jewelry to wear to special events. It provided publicity for the store, and a nice percentage of the time it also supplied sales from indulgent husbands whose wives decided, having once worn the jewels, they couldn't live without them. "Is there a problem?"

"No, not at all. I simply wanted, first of all, to make sure the ball will be going off as scheduled."

He felt slighted, she realized, because she hadn't informed him of the event herself. Instead, he had probably read it in the paper last week along with everyone else. He had reason to be miffed. These occasions did cause him extra work. She made a mental note to make arrangements with Judith so that it wouldn't happen again. "I'm sorry I haven't had time to speak with you before, but everything is falling into place beautifully. The ball should be a big success."

"In that case, the second reason I wanted to speak with you this morning was to give you first opportunity to choose from our inventory. I have an exquisite emerald necklace that you should definitely consider. It would go beautifully with your ring."

He gestured toward the Colombian square-cut emerald on her hand that her father had given her on her twenty-first birthday. "That's very considerate of you to think of me, Mr. Breckinridge, but I won't need anything from the store."

His forehead lifted. "Then you're not attending?"

"No, no, I will definitely be there. But I've decided to wear one of the sets from the vault, the rubies that belonged to Leonora Deverell. I fell in love with them when I first saw them, and their unique red-violet color stayed with me. Luckily I found some material to complement the color, and I've had a ballgown specially made to wear with them."

Obvious distress overrode the formality of his tone. "Are you sure it's wise to wear them?"

"Why wouldn't it be? You saw to the cleaning and repair of the whole Deverell collection just three months ago, right after Caitlin and I inspected them. The rubies are all right, aren't they?"

His already rigid spine straightened. "Most certainly. All of the Deverell jewelry has been checked and their appraisals updated. I was thinking of something else entirely."

"What?"

He took a step closer to the desk. "The Deverell rubies are so extraordinary with their violet cast and the fact that they are perfectly matched. The necklace is one-of-a-kind, really. Its value as a work of art alone is incomparable. And then there are the earrings and the bracelet." He waved a vague hand. "I could never live with myself if anything happened to them, and I'm not sure security is sufficient—"

"Security," she said, taking the word and mulling it over thoughtfully. "You're quite right, Mr. Breckinridge. Perhaps additional security would be a good idea."

He closed the distance to the desk and bent toward her, his expression earnest. "Security can do only so much. I can't help but worry—"

She lifted her hand, effectively cutting off his protest. If it had been any other day, she would have given him all the time in the world to express his views, but not *this* day. "I know how seriously you take your responsibilities, and I can't tell you how much I appreciate it. I would be as appalled as you, perhaps more so, if anything happened to the rubies." She arched a dark brow as a gentle chastisement to Breckinridge for thinking she would be irresponsible, plus as a

reminder to him that she had every right to wear
the jewelry. "I can assure you every contingency
will be covered. Caitlin and I discussed it before
she left for Europe. Jewels as exquisite as those
in the bank vault should be worn and enjoyed,
not hidden away. The rubies belonged to Leonora
Deverell, who, as I'm sure you know, was my
great-great grandmother. It's very exciting for me
to be wearing something that belonged to her,
particularly something so beautiful."

He straightened and backed away from the
desk. "Very well, Miss DiFrenza."

She noted the heavy lacing of disapproval in his
voice and determinedly gave him a bright smile.
"We're going to make a great deal of money for
the Children's Fund and have a lot of fun in the
bargain. Can I count on you?"

"Of course. And if you will see to the necessary
bank authorization, I'll be glad to retrieve the
rubies for you. Then, as I've done in the past, I
will accompany all the jewels to the site of the
ball, stay until after it's over, and see to it they
are all returned safely here."

"Thank you. That will be a great help and one
less thing I have to worry about."

With a nod, he left, and she rose and shut the
door behind him. Once more back at her desk,
she returned her gaze to the phone.

She was sure Amarillo would be in his office by
now. Should she call him? Their kisses had been
tumultuous and so hot, she was surprised they
hadn't burned the fog away. But the fog had
stayed, enclosing them, concealing them. They

could have made love right there and no one would have known.

Except the two of them.

With a moan of distress she dropped her head into her hand. She was incredibly lucky it hadn't happened, she told herself. She simply wished *she* had been the one to break it off instead of Amarillo.

Her pride had been badly damaged. She still could not believe he had broken away from her so abruptly, then walked away with barely a word. Her system had gone into shock and had not recovered. And there was no way they could simply forget last night and go about their business as if it had never happened. Dammit, *she* couldn't. Not without a word of explanation.

She reached for the phone. It rang.

"Angelica DiFrenza." A silence followed her statement. She was trying to decide whether to hang up or repeat her name when she heard Amarillo speak.

"Good morning, Angelica. How are you?"

Her stomach clenched and unclenched. Inconsequentially, she remembered that she had rushed out of the house without breakfast. She would have to make do with the candy bars in her desk drawer. "I'm fine."

"Good." There was a long pause. "Angelica, I called to apologize about last night, and I wanted you to know that I take full responsibility."

She was stunned. Whatever she had expected, it certainly wasn't an apology. Her blood pressure began to rise. "That's extremely gallant of you. By the way, what exactly are you taking responsibility for? The coffee? The fog? It can't be the food. That was Beau Hamilton's doing."

"You know exactly what I'm talking about. That kiss—it never should have happened. It was a mistake."

She sat forward in her chair, and her hand tightened around the receiver. "And why is that, Amarillo? Did you hate kissing me so much?"

"*No.* Of course not. But—"

"Then you did enjoy kissing me?"

"Stop it, Angelica."

"I think it's a pretty easy question. Did you or didn't you?"

He gave a low-throated groan. "You know I did."

The knuckles of the hand holding the phone turned white. "Then why are you calling it a mistake?"

"Because it was."

"Would you like to explain that to me?"

"It—it's complicated."

Something was hurting near her heart. Absently, she picked up a pencil and began playing with it. "It's complicated. It's a mistake. I see. By the way, I totally agree with you."

"Dammit, I should never have kissed you!"

The pencil snapped in two. Tears welled in her eyes. "Kiss me? What you *did*, Amarillo, was nearly undress me. Then you caressed my breast as if you were dying to feel me. Now that I think about it, you said you'd been wanting to do it forever. I know it was a line said in the heat of passion, but it was very effective. You really should be congratulated on it. You took my nipple into your mouth. You—you made me feel things that—" She stopped and squeezed her eyes shut, absolutely appalled at what she had said.

"Angelica?"

She opened her eyes but didn't see anything. "I accept your apology," she said woodenly. "Don't give the matter another thought."

He uttered a potent expletive. "I have a day filled with meetings, but I'll cancel—"

"It's not that important, Amarillo."

He uttered another curse beneath his breath. "Meet me tonight at my place, seven o'clock. We need to talk about what happened." His normal, growllike way of speaking sounded rawer, rougher, as if he had gargled with gravel.

"Why? So that you can smooth last night over and make me believe it never happened?"

"I'm not that good, honey."

Her skin tingled at the endearment, and her lips firmed with displeasure. No matter what he said, she was sure his purpose was to ensure that in the future when they saw each other, she wouldn't remember she would have made love with him on the hood of her car if he had wanted to. Just thinking about it made her flush red with embarrassment. "I can't think of one single reason why we should meet."

"Because I want to—how's that for a reason?"

"Selfish."

"Angelica, it would probably be much better for you if we never saw each other again, but we both know that's very near impossible."

"Because of Nico."

"Because of last night, *dammit.*"

Judith stuck her head in the door, waved good morning, then shut the door again.

"Please, Angelica."

She didn't think she had ever heard him say please to anyone unless it was a waiter or a waitress. She was tired, she realized, and the day hadn't even begun. She wanted nothing more than to see him again; and on the other hand, she couldn't think of anything worse than seeing him again. "All right."

"Seven o'clock."

As the day passed, Angelica's energy grew, and so did her nerves. By the time she knocked on Amarillo's door at seven that evening, she was a basket case. As soon as he opened the door and stepped aside to allow her to enter, her doubts about the wisdom of coming expanded until she thought she would choke with them.

There was an emotional danger in simply being near him. On some level there always had been. Tonight the danger seemed to be intensified by the jeans molding his strong thighs and the gold shirt opened at the collar and leaving bare his strong brown throat.

Outside, twilight had fallen. Inside, a single light softly illuminated a circled area that included a green cut-velvet couch. But she chose not to sit. Relaxing even a little was out of the question.

To her overly charged senses, the interior of the large warehouse seemed layered with intimacy, and the air was absolutely electric. She could feel herself withdrawing, pulling her emotions inward, trying to lessen the chance that in some way he might affect her as he had last night. She was convinced one touch from him and she would go up in flames. It was her greatest fear.

"I'm sorry this is so awkward for you," he said suddenly.

Startled, she looked up and saw him watching her. She wondered what kind of expression had been on her face. "For me? This isn't awkward for you?"

"Of course it is. Hell, *awkward* doesn't even begin to cover it." He took several steps away, then turned and came back.

He reminded her of a caged wildcat, she thought. The muscles of his body were coiled and tensed, the angles of his face were sharp, almost diamond-edged, his hands were balled into fists. She didn't think she had ever seen him less than calm and self-possessed. Except last night.

"Just do me a favor, Amarillo. Don't apologize to me again."

He stopped, and she found his stillness even more threatening than his movement.

"I have to do something, Angelica. If not an apology, then something. We've got to settle this."

"I don't know what you mean by *settle* this," she said carefully, "and I don't know what you want from me."

"Want?" A strange expression flickered over his face. He reached out a hand toward her, then quickly pulled it back. "I don't want to hurt you."

He easily could if she let him, she thought, and immediately denied it. "You're giving yourself an awful lot of credit."

He rubbed his eyes with a thumb and finger, then looked at her again. "This isn't going well, is it? Let's start over."

"You mean like, 'Hello, Amarillo. How are you? Nice night.' What would that accomplish?"

"You were angry this morning when we talked. I don't want to leave it at anger."

She laughed incredulously. "And *that's* why you asked me to come over here this evening? Please, Amarillo. I'm a big girl now. I can get over being angry all by myself. And if you're worried about Nico, don't be. He stopped defending my honor long ago."

"Nico is the last thing on my mind, believe me."

"What's the first?"

He sent her a look that nearly seared the skin from her bones.

"You know what?" she asked shakily. "I still don't understand what happened last night, but I'm not up for a post mortem. Maybe it would be best to think of it as an aberration. For some reason, we acted irrationally, and the whole thing was a quirk, a peculiar happening, an abnormality. Perhaps the moon was in the wrong position."

"There wasn't any moon, Angelica."

"There was a moon," she said with determination. "We couldn't see it.

"We couldn't see it because we were too busy looking at each other."

"We couldn't see it because of the fog," she said explosively. "Why are you being obstinate? I just gave you a nice justification for what happened. It may not be the best justification possible, and it may not make perfect sense, but I can live with it."

"Dammit, it won't wash, and you know it."

The gold of his eyes glittered in the growing dark. Warmth spread along her skin. She walked to a table and switched on a light. "I think I should go."

"I've always known kissing you would be like that," he said, his tone and expression brooding.

She was thrown off balance. "Like what?"

"Like pure fire."

"Then why hadn't you ever kissed me before?"

"Because," he said, his voice a hard growl, "I knew it would be like that."

Suddenly it was all too much for her—Amarillo, the puzzle of what had happened between them, the emotions she had felt and was feeling now. Tears flooded her eyes. Embarrassed, she tried to brush them away, but one escaped and slid down her cheek.

"Lord, Angelica, don't cry." He drew in a deep, ragged breath, fighting the urge to take her into his arms and comfort her. But if he did . . .

She quickly pulled herself together. "Don't worry, I'm not going to embarrass you by crying. And something else I'm not going to do is stay here a minute longer. You haven't said one thing since I've been here that's made any sense, and—"

He drove his fingers through his hair. "Dammit, you're right, and I think I'll stop trying."

The air turned flammable in the space of a second, and the suddenness of the change left her without defense. Her heart pounded, heat began to twist through her insides. All of that—and nothing had happened yet.

Then he moved, coming toward her, intent in

every taut line and muscle of his body, a predator with one thing on his mind: Her.

She felt as if the breath had been squeezed from her lungs. She struggled for air, for resolve, for determination that would make her turn and leave. She didn't stir from where she was.

He halted in front of her, and the heat sparking off his body touched her and started her burning.

He reached out his hands and framed her face. "Do you have any idea how beautiful I think you are?"

His deep voice rolled over her, through her— a crashing wave of heated emotion. Something momentous was about to happen, an explosion was building, and she felt helpless to stop it. Her lips parted. "You think I'm beautiful?"

He shifted his weight; somehow he was closer to her. "You have no idea."

She felt his breath on her face, his hands on her skin. She tilted her head back and gazed up at him. His golden eyes were ablaze.

"What do you feel like on the inside?" he whispered.

A cry left her lips. He captured the sound with his, and then he was kissing her with a completeness she felt to her toes. She didn't think she'd ever had such a kiss before. It was a possession, a ravagement, and, she sensed, it was only a small preview of the lovemaking that would come. Her legs turned to water at the thought.

He pulled his mouth from hers to graze his lips up and down the smooth, silky skin of her neck. "What do you feel like on the inside?" he asked again. "Am I going to be able to stand it or am I going to go up in flames and be consumed?"

She had no answer and he didn't expect one, she realized with a thrill. Neither one of them had any control over what was about to happen. The course of a hurricane couldn't be changed. A tornado couldn't be made to turn in the opposite direction. She and Amarillo could not be stopped.

"I think I'll go up in flames," he muttered roughly, answering his own question. He reached behind her and unzipped her dress, then he swung her into his arms and strode to the sofa. He put her down, and came down next to her. Passion gripped his body, frustration hammered in his head. There were things he should think about, do, say, but something primitive was driving him. The process of undressing became an excruciating task. He couldn't bear the intricacies of hooks and buttons or wasted time.

"These damn clothes." He pulled at her dress, managing finally to slide the top of it from her shoulders and halfway down her arms. Similar effort managed to get her panties off. Then he parted from her for only a moment to undo his jeans, push them down his hips and free himself.

She tried to help, attempting to unbutton his shirt, but in her hurry she ended up tearing buttons off. It didn't matter. Her hands discovered his chest and the springy texture of the hair that covered the broad expanse.

They were tangled together, arms, legs, clothes. His patience was in threads. His hand found the softness of her thighs and higher. He touched her and heard her give a quick gasp of pleasure. He nearly lost control then, but he forced himself to hold on. Probing further, he found the tiny, sensitive cleft. Her hips began to lift and circle. In his loins, pressure wound tighter, heat became molten. He slipped long fingers into her.

"*Amarillo!*" Her hands clenched his shoulders, her nails dug into his flesh.

She was velvety soft, temptingly hot, deliciously damp. His teeth bared in agony. "Lord, Angelica, I don't think I can wait."

"Don't. Don't."

Her plea of urgency was his final undoing. "I *can't.*"

He thrust into her, and she cried out as her senses exploded with new, more powerful feelings of ecstasy. He surged in and out of her, and she matched him movement for movement. It was hot and savage, and pleasure swept through her like a rampaging river. She couldn't think, couldn't catch her breath. Something was building within her, something unbearable, something uncivilized. She clutched frantically at him and called his name.

With a deep, guttural groan he lifted her hips and thrust deeper into her. Once. Twice. He felt her tense beneath him, then her body began to shudder and contract around him. Control fled, and a fine madness overcame him. He cried out hoarsely and drove into her one final time.

When next she woke, she was being carried up the stairs. "Amarillo?"

He kissed the top of her head. "Shhh, go back to sleep. I'm taking you to bed."

She pressed her face into his chest and inhaled the musky scent of his body. "I should go home," she murmured.

"Morning's soon enough."

With a barely audible sigh she gave herself up to the warmth of his arms. There was no one at home waiting for her, no one who would be worried. Perhaps he was right. She would sleep here. With him.

When he lowered her to the bed, she gazed up at him. Through a huge arched window behind the ebony headboard, moonlight streamed, gilding his hair and half-bare body.

He rested one knee on the bed. "We never did manage to get undressed."

"No, we didn't." Her gaze traveled to his jeans that hung low on his hips, unfastened, unzipped. Heat surged through her. Feeling suddenly vulnerable, she sat up and scooted backward until she was against the pillows.

He took the place beside her, leaning back against the headboard. She looked unbelievably sensuous and erotic, with her hair tousled, her clothes disheveled, her lips swollen and pouty. "I was right," he murmured huskily.

"About what?"

"I did go up in flames."

She wet her bottom lip with the tip of her tongue and whispered. "I did too."

With a groan he reached for her and brought her across his lap. She adjusted her legs so that she was astride him.

He felt her pressing down on him, warm and moist. Instantaneously his body caught fire and his mind began to haze over. "Dammit, this time I'm at least going to get your clothes off you." He skimmed her dress up her body, over her head, and tossed it aside. Her bra and slip followed.

And then he was inside her, so simply, so easily, so mind-bendingly wonderfully that he wondered why he had let his obsession with getting her undressed delay him.

When his hands fastened on her breasts, he remembered and understood why he had wanted to delay. He had a deeply primitive need to feel every inch of her skin, both inside and out. He clasped her hips and began moving her in a circular motion, and at the same time began to thrust up into her.

She felt filled with him. No part of her remained unaffected. Powerful sensations swept through her time after time, threatening to carry her away in the maelstrom of ecstasy. She reached behind him and grasped the ebony headboard to brace herself as she undulated against him, uncaringly plunging herself deeper into the dark, sweet mire of passion that Amarillo offered.

The moonlight streamed in the window behind him, highlighting Angelica. She looked like pure passion to him, with her head back, her hair streaming down her back, her lips swollen from his kisses, her face intent yet softened with desire.

He bent his head and captured a nipple and pulled on it. Sweat beaded his brow, his muscles hurt from the restraint he had imposed on himself. She was driving him mad. He had never known lovemaking to grip him like this, to take possession of him so completely that he couldn't consider the consequences, couldn't consider anything but the deep, gut-wrenching, soul-satisfying completion that was fast approaching for both of them. The sounds she made and the tension he felt in her body told him she was with him all the way.

"Let's do it now," he muttered hoarsely.

She gasped out her agreement. "Now."

He tightened his grip on her buttocks, and his movements turned more urgent, more fierce and savage. He didn't know how much more he would be able to stand of the incredible fiery pleasure. There was the risk that he might combust, and take her with him.

And then the risk became a reality. And the reality became a fantasy that went on and on.

Four

The deep, steady breathing of the man lying beside her startled Angelica into wakefulness just before dawn. She listened, at first somewhat bemused. The sound was foreign to her; she wasn't used to having a man in her bed.

Then she remembered.

She wasn't in *her* bed.

She closed her eyes as the preceding night's events came rushing back to her. She had come to the warehouse so that she and Amarillo could discuss their first kiss—the kiss that had been so out of character for them both, the kiss that had gotten completely out of control, the kiss that had turned into another and another. her hope had been they would be able to place what had happened between the two of them into some sort of perspective, and then put the incident behind them.

Instead, their talk had turned into a firestorm

of lovemaking that had continued all night. And still she knew no more about Amarillo now than she had when she'd stood by her car and watched him walk away from her. He remained, as ever, an enigma.

At the same time, she had no idea what was going on with her. Each time he touched her, she went up in flames. What kind of sense did that make? She had known him for years. She could find no explanation. A prudent retreat, she decided, was the only answer.

It was the feeling of emptiness that awakened Amarillo as the first golden rays of the day's sun began to filter through the window behind him.

His hand shot out to the place beside him. The sheets were cool. Unoccupied. Abandoned.

He clenched his hand into a fist and slammed it into the bed. *Damn!*

Angelica walked into her bedroom that evening, kicked off her shoes, and shrugged out of her suit jacket. She was exhausted, but she headed straight for her closet and her luggage. Sometime during the day she had decided that she would leave for SwanSea the next day. She had labored feverishly to finish as much of her work as possible. As for the work she had been unable to complete, she had decided that what could not be handled from SwanSea could wait until her return. She needed to get out of town.

Amarillo had not tried to see her or talk with

her that day, but she had decided not to worry about what he was thinking or feeling. More than likely he was very embarrassed about the previous night. He might even blame the whole situation on her in some way. He had obviously decided to stay away from her. In any event, he was impenetrable as granite. It would take dynamite to blow him apart and see what was inside him, and she simply didn't feel up to using explosives.

It had been a night of wonder to her. Together they had traveled to heights she had never dreamed possible. She knew she would never be the same, either emotionally or physically.

But she had to go on with her life.

It wasn't in her to dismiss lightly what had happened between them, nor could she forget it. But what she could do was to view the whole thing as a freak occurrence, and, in addition, physically *leave* the situation.

She set about packing with a vengeance, and sometime later, when she heard the doorbell ring, her task was nearly completed.

On her way to answer the bell, she cast a satisfied glance at the red-violet ballgown that had been delivered earlier in the evening. It was in a plastic bag and ready to be laid on the backseat of her car for the following day's trip.

Downstairs she stood on her stockinged feet to peer through the door's security peephole. What she saw made her pulse pound into overdrive.

Amarillo was on her porch, a scowl of anger on his face.

She straightened and pressed suddenly shaking fingers to her forehead, undecided what she should do. She felt extremely stupid, because for some reason that totally escaped her at the moment he was the last person she had expected to see on her doorstep.

The bell rang the second time. Her mind cleared. There was really only one course of action open to her. She let him in.

"About time," he said, stepping into the entry hall. "What took you so long?"

She closed the door and folded her hands across her breasts. "Hello, Amarillo. Why are you here?"

"It's not obvious?"

The sharpness of his voice stabbed at her, attempting to cut into her. His anger must have been simmering all day, she thought, and definitely had something to do with the previous night. She just wished she knew what so that she could prepare herself. She turned and started down the hall. "Come into the living room."

"Why do you look so tired?" he asked as they entered a spacious, elegantly furnished room.

"Maybe because I am. Look, why don't you go ahead and get whatever it is that's bothering you off your chest so that I can get to bed early tonight."

His hands flipped back his jacket before they settled on his hips. "Whatever it is that's *bothering* me? Lady, you are one cool customer. We just spent a night joined together in the hottest, sweatiest, most intimate ways imaginable, and you ask what's *bothering* me?"

She swallowed and discovered a hard lump had settled in her throat. "So then, can I gather from that outburst that you're upset because we had sex last night?"

His eyes narrowed slightly, as if, she thought uneasily, he were trying to gain a better focus and see into her mind.

"You're not?"

His deep growling tone made her want to seek shelter. She rolled her shoulders in a casual shrug and felt a twinge of pain, her first indication that she'd been holding herself rigidly. "I decided not to let myself get upset. We got into trouble when we tried to pursue what happened with the kiss. There's no telling what would happen if we tried to pursue the rationale behind last night."

"Last night." He shook his head, and for a moment she thought she saw amazement on his face. "Last night," he said, continuing. "I want you to know, Angelica, that I didn't intend for anything to happen."

Somehow that didn't make her feel better. "No, I don't suppose you did."

"But on the other hand, I'm not sorry it happened."

Now she felt better. "Thank you for saying so."

"I mean it."

She nodded, appreciating his kindness. It made her all the more determined to get on with her life—something she was sure she would not be able to do if they made love again. Lord, where had such a thought come from, she wondered.

There was no chance of that happening, though. His purpose there was obviously to try to let her down easy. But to her chagrin, she was discovering she could not take his polite, gentle dismissal easily.

She felt as if he had flung her off a cliff last night when he had taken her into his arms, and now she was about to crash on the rocks below. To come out of this in one piece, she had to go on the offensive, soften the landing.

"Why did you leave without telling me?" he asked, his voice lowering into its purr.

Once again he had managed to throw her off balance, she thought, dismayed. "I woke up and decided it was time to leave."

"But why didn't you tell me?"

"You were sleeping deeply. I thought it would be rude to wake you."

He rarely slept deeply, he thought, but then, he couldn't remember ever staying up all night and making love. And he almost always awoke alone. But this morning, when he had awakened and found her gone, he had been deeply disturbed.

He averted his gaze from her. Just being near her had his blood heating. He couldn't seem to look at her too long without wanting to kiss her until she was senseless and then undress them both and repeat last night down to the finest detail. How in hell had he managed to keep his hands off her for so many years? He wished he knew. All this time he must have been walking a tightrope without realizing the enormity of his feat.

"It was a mistake," she was saying. "It shouldn't have happened."

His gaze flew back to her. "That's damned ironic. A day ago I said the same thing about the kiss, and you got angry. Now you're saying last night was a mistake, and *I'm* angry as hell. Our opinions have reversed. How did that happen?"

She threw up her hands. "This is pointless. I'm not the one with the answers. However, I am the one who's tired. Please, leave."

He suddenly grabbed her arms and pulled her to him. "Dammit, we ignite whenever we're near each other, Angelica! I want to know why! After all these years, *why*?"

She couldn't think. Being in contact with his hard, muscled body put her in a type of peril with which she could not cope. At this moment the contact seemed an even greater peril than the rocks she was hurtling toward. With an immense burst of energy she broke free of his grip. Taking shuddering breaths, she forcibly pushed air into her lungs. "I told you I don't know the answers, and we don't seem to be able to have a sensible discussion about it, or anything else, for that matter. So stay away from me, and I'll stay away from you."

He didn't like her response at all. "And you think *that's* going to solve everything?"

"Yes, yes, I do."

He stared at her, clenching and unclenching his hands. Dammit, he couldn't get a handle on what was happening, and it was driving him crazy. She had been on the edge of his life for years, and now she was square in the middle of it. He wasn't sure he had the strength to shove her back to the edge, and staying away from her seemed an intolerable solution to the problem.

"You weren't a virgin," he said softly.

Her breath caught in her throat; she pointed a shaking finger at him. "You're going to have to stop doing that."

"What?"

"Making unexpected statements straight out of left field."

"I'm sorry," he said, looking anything but contrite. "It's just that I didn't know you had slept with anyone."

"Why in heaven's name should you know?" she asked, incensed. "That's a very personal, private matter."

"And last night we were together in a very personal, private way." His eyes glittered like beautiful hard stones. "Wouldn't you say, Angelica?"

"What I would say is that last night is over with."

He took a few steps away, then turned and returned to the spot where he had been standing. "We see each other often enough so I pretty much know whom you've dated through the years. But there's never been anyone I've seen you with that I thought you might sleep with. Not even the jerk you almost became engaged to."

"Roger wasn't a jerk."

"He was a jerk."

She sighed inwardly. Amarillo was tenacious as a bulldog, and she wasn't up to a struggle. She held up a hand in surrender. "Gary McKee. I had a short affair with Gary McKee. Okay?"

A muscle in his jaw jerked. He could barely manage to get the name out, and his words positively stung with sarcasm. "I never met a Gary McKee."

"That's because you were in Texas."

"When? Which time?"

She wrapped her arms around her waist. "When you took Rebecca Randolph with you to show her where you grew up and to meet your relatives. I thought you must be pretty serious about her because you had never taken any other woman, but you came back alone."

His expression turned strange and unreadable. "Rebecca and I were only casual friends. She was going to Texas because her family was living in Austin at the time. I offered her a ride in my plane, since I was going there anyway. I touched down at the Austin airport, let her off, and within fifteen minutes I was airborne again, on my way to Lubbock, alone."

She stared at him as a horrible thought occurred to her. Could it be remotely possible that she had thrown herself into an affair with someone, who in the end had meant nothing to her, because she had believed Amarillo had finally found a woman who made him want to marry again? She remembered now that her affair had ended about the same time he had returned from Texas without Rebecca. By turns, she went hot and cold. It was extremely unnerving to think it possible she had not been conscious of the true reason why she had done something.

He raised his hand toward her. "Angelica—"

The phone rang.

She started at the shrill noise. It rang again. After a moment she walked to the phone and answered. "Hello."

"You shouldn't go out with blond-haired men.

You shouldn't go out at all. You had better start minding me or I'll have to punish you."

The high-pitched, muffled voice went through her like a knife. The phone slipped through her nerveless fingers and slid to the floor. Amarillo was instantly by her side.

"What's wrong?" he asked even as he picked up the receiver and held it to his ear. "The line's dead. Who was it?" He replaced the receiver in its cradle.

She gave a hollow laugh. "He thinks your hair is blond. How silly."

His brows knitted with concern and confusion. "Who does?"

"The man who keeps calling. Your hair is sandy, not blond, but he said it was blond."

He put his arm around her, led her to the nearest sofa, and pulled her down beside him. "Okay, now tell me what's going on. Who is the man who keeps calling? And what does he say?"

She exhaled a breath and drew in another one. "It's really nothing."

"*Nothing* wouldn't upset you. The call did."

"Yes, and that's just it. I shouldn't let the calls affect me. He's only some crank."

"Calls? How many times has he called you?"

"Four." The number startled her. She hadn't realized it had been so many times. "I guess that's right. Four. The first was here, two nights ago, right before Nico phoned. The second was the next morning at work. The third was in the evening, here again. And now this one."

"And what does he say?"

She shrugged. "He keeps telling me to mind

him, to stay home, to not go out, to be a good girl. That sort of thing. Just then he said I shouldn't go out with blond-haired men. It's ridiculous when you think about it."

"Have you told your father? Why in hell haven't you told me before?"

"No, I haven't told my father and for the same reason I haven't told you. Because it didn't seem important." And it hadn't, but now she was vaguely surprised to realize she was relieved he knew.

Amarillo geared up for action. "There are things that can be done. And the first thing is to place a trace on both your home and office phones."

"No, no. It's too much trouble. He may not even call again. Remember about five years ago when you and Nico were still on the police force and I began getting crank calls?"

He nodded. "Nico came unglued."

"And you were there right along beside him."

His gaze was cool. "What's your point?"

"The two of you brought to bear as much technology and police department weight as you could manage trying to trace and locate whoever was doing it. Remember?"

"I remember. We were never able to catch the bastard."

"And the person finally stopped calling. Since then, I've had other calls, usually right after my picture has appeared in the paper, as it did last week."

"Did you tell Nico about the other calls?"

"No way. The two of you insisted I stay here in the house under guard the first time it happened.

I couldn't even go to the store. They had to messenger my work to me. It was awful." A shudder went through her.

He frowned. "Why would that upset you? You had everything you needed here."

"But I couldn't walk out my own front door if I wanted to," she said with real distress. "I have to be able to get out of a place if I want to."

He didn't understand the fear he saw in her eyes; more than that, he didn't understand why her fear should hurt him so. "Sounds like a form of claustrophobia."

"Call it what you will, it doesn't matter. I vowed never again to allow my life to be interrupted like that. The calls are a nuisance, but they eventually stop. This guy, whoever he is, will too."

He leaned forward, his expression intent. "Listen to me, Angelica. You're right, up to a point. A great majority of calls like this are harmless, but that doesn't mean you shouldn't take every precaution possible. And in case you haven't figured it out yet, this guy is watching you."

A cold chill slid down her spine.

"How else would he know that you were seeing a blond-haired man?" he added quietly.

Her lips firmed into a stubborn line. "I still say he'll get tired and go away soon. He'll find someone else's picture in the paper and bother them for a while. And there'll be someone after that."

"You may be right about this guy being harmless. I hope you are. But I don't take anything for granted. And until your theory proves out, you are going to have bodyguards round the clock and your home and office phones tapped."

She surged to her feet. "No bodyguards. Absolutely not."

He copied her, coming to his feet as quickly as she. "Yes, absolutely. If you think for one minute I'm going to stand by and do nothing while some bastard harasses you, think again."

She lashed out without thought. "Since when did you become my protector?"

"Nico—"

"Forget Nico," she said heatedly. "He's not here."

"Exactly."

"Oh, I see. You're taking over the role of big brother. Well, you can forget it." The idea was abhorrent to her, but at the moment she couldn't think why.

"The role of big brother is probably a damned sight better and safer role than the one I played all last night!" He stared at her, noting her stricken look, then plunged rigid fingers through his hair. "*Damn*, why do I let you get to me?"

She held up a shaking hand. "Okay, let's stop this. This argument about bodyguards and phone taps is academic anyway. I'm leaving for SwanSea first thing in the morning."

He stilled, his volatile energy and power suddenly, frighteningly, contained. "When did you make your decision?"

"Today. It seems like the thing to do."

"And did telling me enter anywhere into your plans?"

"I would have told you." She paused. "If you had asked. Anyway, I was already scheduled to go there in a few days. I'm only stepping up my plans."

"And how much of this sudden decision has to do with me?"

Lying to him would have been an easy solution. Unfortunately it was beyond her at the moment. "Just about everything."

"We're not through, Angelica. You know that, don't you? We haven't settled a thing."

She tried to laugh, but couldn't even come close. "There's that word again. *Settled.* We never get anywhere with it. Like I said before, we can't even carry on a normal, sensible conversation. I say we give up."

"Can you? I can't." Without warning, glints of heat appeared in the depths of his golden eyes.

An unbidden warmth swept over her, adding to her turmoil. And, she realized, she had begun to develop a headache. "It's late. I have a long drive tomorrow. I want you to leave now."

"I'm going with you."

"Where?" she asked, unable to follow his rapid-fire mind.

"SwanSea."

She gasped. "SwanSea? I asked you to come, and you said you couldn't. Remember? You said with Nico out of the country—"

"I changed my mind."

"Just like that?"

"Just like that."

He appeared utterly controlled. She didn't trust him. "Why, Amarillo?"

"The Children's Fund is an excellent charity. It's been a while since I've been up there. I need to check on my horses. I need a break. Pick any one, and you'll have a legitimate reason."

"You changed your mind because you suddenly think I need protecting, and I won't have it."

"You have no choice."

His soft voice was like cold steel.

She whirled away, strode into the entry hall, and jerked open the front door. "I can't keep you from going to SwanSea, but I can keep you from going with me. Don't even try to come by here in the morning."

"I was thinking I could fly us up," he said, sauntering into the hall.

"I'm driving."

"All the more reason for us to fly. You drive like a maniac."

"I'm driving. Alone."

He paused at the door and looked down at her. "Okay, Angelica, you win the point. Drive up alone if you like. But when you arrive, look behind you, because I'll be there. Whatever the reason, I can't seem to let you go off without me." He smiled slowly. "And maybe it won't be so bad. Maybe we'll actually manage to have a few normal talks that won't end in lovemaking. Maybe."

She slammed the door after him, not knowing whether he had left her with a threat or a promise and uncertain which she would prefer.

Five

That night Angelica dreamt, but in the morning she could only remember snatches of the dream—a sweet voice saying, "be good," the same voice saying, "my golden-haired boy."

Her dreams had begun to leave her with an eerie feeling, and she didn't know why. Last night's caller had said blond-haired man. Had her brain in some way short-circuited the phrase and come up with golden-haired boy? She didn't even know why the dream was still on her mind. She had certainly never been bothered before by the contents of her dreams. It was silly when she stopped to think about it. Still . . .

She shook off the sensation that something was wrong and had a large slice of the Chocolate Angelica for breakfast. Afterward, she froze the rest of the gateau, phoned her father to say good-bye, threw her luggage into the car, and headed north out of Boston.

She had been driving less than an hour when she noticed the sleek, shiny black Corvette in her rearview mirror that was following her, *had* been following her, she realized now, almost from the first. Amarillo, of course.

Her first impulse was to jam the accelerator to the floorboard and get away from him, but it was an impulse quickly squelched. The last thing she needed was another speeding ticket on her already tainted record. Besides, common sense told her she would never be able to out-drive or out-speed Amarillo's car. So she set her speedometer at a safe four and a half miles over the speed limit and drove on.

The signs and scenery whizzed by, and it soon became obvious to her that although she had managed to keep Amarillo out of her car, she couldn't keep him out of her thoughts.

In his words, they *ignited* whenever they were together. He kept asking her questions about their situation, wanting to know what she thought. But if he had an explanation or an opinion as to why or even as to what they should do about it, he was keeping it to himself.

She might as well admit it to herself: she had relished each moment of their incredible lovemaking. Only in the aftermath had she found herself with unsettled emotions and unsatisfied questions. And the whole thing was making her crazy.

As a young girl she had loved roller coasters. But as a twenty-seven-year-old woman involved in some sort of crazy relationship with an infuriatingly enigmatic man, she had discovered she hated the roller coaster of emotions she was on.

She had to get off. She had to stay away from the man who had put her on it.

She glanced in the rearview mirror and grimaced. The black car still held its position a reasonable distance behind her, but there was something very predatory about it, with its hungry-for-speed lines and look. It wasn't crowding her, but like a true predator, it kept pursuing.

When she turned her car onto the long drive that wound up to SwanSea, she was relieved. Between her mental anguishing and the constant view of the black car in the mirror she was ready for the trip to be over.

As always, her first sight of the great house touched a cord in her. It wasn't the immensity of SwanSea that impressed her, nor the staggering wealth it represented. Rather, it was the "soul" of the house: the strength and indomitability she sensed woven through the stone, mortar, and wood of it. And most of all the sensation that this was a place she belonged. She never tired of her visits and always regretted their end.

Through the windshield she saw the tall, silver-haired manager, Winston Lawrence, standing by the drive, waiting for her. She smiled and waved.

"How do you do it, Mr. Lawrence?" she asked as soon as she had stopped the car and slid out. "You're always here waiting for me when I arrive, yet usually I notify you only of the date of my arrival. How do you know the exact moment when I will be coming up the drive?"

He smiled warmly. "You wouldn't want me to give away all my secrets, would you? Otherwise I could be replaced."

She laughed, enjoying the sound of his crisp British accent. "No one could ever replace you. Not in a million years. In fact, the whole family would fight to the death any hotel or resort that tried to get you away from us."

His smile broadened with pleasure. "I can assure you death won't be necessary. I have no intention of leaving. Once a person has managed SwanSea, everything else seems second-rate." As he heard another car approaching, he darted a glance down the drive. "Is that Mr. Smith?"

"Yes, I'm afraid it is," she said, thinking with disgust that the man and his car had similar purring growls. She strolled around her car and opened the trunk. Peter, one of the bellmen who had worked at SwanSea since its opening, came running up to get her luggage. "Hello, Peter, how have you been?"

"Fine, Miss DiFrenza. It's great to have you back with us."

"It's great to be back," she said with sincerity.

Behind her she heard Mr. Lawrence say, "Mr. Smith, what an unexpected surprise. We didn't anticipate your arrival."

"I'm sorry for not calling ahead," Amarillo drawled, "but the trip was a last-minute decision. Do you think you can find room for me?"

Mr. Lawrence chuckled. "No apologies are necessary. I hope you know you are always welcome. And as a matter of fact, you and Miss DiFrenza will be the only two on the fourth floor. You can keep each other company, and you can have any room you wish, except for the one designated as hers, of course."

Amarillo smiled, and she felt its effect as a tingling on her skin.

"My usual room will be fine," he said.

Angelica decided to take it easy for the rest of the day and see if she couldn't ease the strain she had begun to notice in herself. She walked for a while, visiting all her favorite places, then took a swim. Later she caught sight of Amarillo when she strayed too near the stables. She quickly corrected that mistake by changing direction.

She was feeling quite relaxed that evening around ten when she answered the door and found Amarillo.

"You didn't come down to dinner," he said. "Is everything all right?"

"Yes." In a glance she took in the western cut of his dark dinner jacket and pants. He exuded enough raw, earthy sensuality for ten men, she thought sourly, and tightened the belt of the short violet silk robe that matched the chemise beneath. "I didn't feel like dressing for dinner, that's all."

Without invitation he stepped into the large room and pushed the door closed. The room had been done in dark woods and different textures of white fabrics. Intricately worked lace dripped over the bed's canopy and down its sides. A matching lace coverlet spread across the bed. A pair of red, slingback, high-heeled shoes lay on their sides by the white marble fireplace where a fire burned. Her perfumed scent seemed to hang in the air. The room reeked of her own particular brand of femininity and sensuality. His expression darkened. "Did you have dinner sent up?"

"Yes. Amarillo, do you think it's a good idea for you to be here?"

His mouth quirked. "Hell, no."

"I don't either."

"So, are you going to ask me to leave?"

The fact that it sounded like a challenge wasn't the reason she hesitated. Rather, she had a far more basic reason. Her skin had warmed as soon as she had opened the door and seen him, yet she was only just now noticing it. That meant her body was getting used to his effect on her. It was a highly disturbing thought. "Look, there's no need to be worried about me. I'm perfectly safe here."

"Maybe." His eyes were hooded, their expression veiled. "At any rate, I didn't come here to discuss the caller. I'm hoping it will be a while before he realizes you've left town. Your luggage wasn't in view when you pulled out of your driveway this morning. If he was watching, I'm sure he thought you went to work as usual. Of course if he's smart, he'll figure out where you are, but you've bought yourself some time. No one followed you here but me." He tugged at his tie until it came loose, unbuttoned several top buttons, then chose a seat on the couch in front of the fireplace.

It was her own fault, she concluded. She never answered his question directly, never told him to leave. She walked around to the front of the couch and perched on the arm. "Should I ask why you *are* here?" Reluctant humor edged her voice.

"To try to have a normal talk that doesn't end in lovemaking—remember?—like I said we would."

She shouldn't have asked.

"And to tell you something."

And she probably shouldn't ask this either. "What's that?"

His gaze skimmed over her. "I like you in violet. I always have."

Shock held her silent for a moment. "That's what you wanted to tell me?"

He nodded. "I've always liked you in violet."

She gave a little laugh. "Now that I think about it, you once told me you liked me in this color, didn't you? I must have been around sixteen."

"You had just turned sixteen, and the dress you were wearing at the time was violet and had sprigs of purple and white flowers embroidered around the neckline and hem. It was your junior prom dress."

She grinned. "A couple of months later Elena and I looked in my closet and found only violet-colored clothes."

Her grin slowly faded as she thought of the leather suit she had worn to dinner with him, the sleep set she had on now, the cotton knit sweater she had packed, even the ballgown she had had made, plus a great number of other items hanging in her closet in Boston.

They were *all* violet.

It seemed as if her mind had been playing tricks on her without her knowing it. She slid off the armrest and onto the couch.

"You were really something as a sixteen-year-old," he said softly, laying his arm along the back of the couch. "You still are."

The temperature of her skin increased; her gaze turned troubled. "Did you know that back then I had a terrible crush on you?"

"No," he said, surprised.

"You remembered the violet dress I bought for the junior prom. Do you also remember that my date stood me up that night?"

"Very well," he said, his tone unexpectedly cold.

"His name was Eddie Hewitt, and he had asked me to go. He was new at school, and I thought he was really neat."

"Neat?"

"Neat," she affirmed. "I took two hours to get ready, then came downstairs and waited two more hours. Nico still lived at home then, and you and he were playing pool in the game room. I decided to wait for Eddie in there with you two. As the night went on, I saw the looks you and Nico exchanged, but I couldn't believe Eddie would stand me up. Just when it was beginning to dawn on me that he wasn't coming, one of my girlfriends called me from the dance to tell me he was there with another girl."

"He'll never know how lucky he was that he was only sixteen," Amarillo drawled. "If he'd been even two years older, your brother and I would have taken him to the nearest dark alley and had a serious discussion with him. As it was—"

"As it was, you were wonderful. You came over to me, put your hands on my shoulders, and kissed me on my cheek. Then you told me that one day Eddie would look back on that night and want to kill himself because he botched the chance of going to the dance with me."

The vertical creases in his cheeks deepened with a show of humor. "There's no doubt about it, and I still believe that. Whatever happened to the little twerp, anyway?"

"I have no idea. His family moved again the following year."

"It's just as well. He wouldn't have had a future in Boston."

"No?" A sudden grin lit her face. "Do you remember what we did that night?"

He thought for a minute, then burst out laughing. "Nico and I took you out for a chocolate sundae."

"I guess I've always had a thing for chocolate." Her voice softened. "You were very nice to me that night, and as I said, I thought you were wonderful."

His smile slowly faded as he watched her use her fingers to comb a portion of her dark hair away from her face. "You were very sweet. It was easy to be nice to you."

The hard lines of his face were softened by the warm glow of the fire. She hesitated, then plunged ahead. "Apparently it later became more difficult for you because you changed with me. You grew more distant."

"You're imagining things."

"No, Amarillo, I've never done that. You don't give a person much room for imagining things where you are concerned. Let's face something here. There may not be another chance. You wanted to talk. Let's *really* talk. What changed,

Amarillo? When I was younger, you were open and friendly toward me. But as I grew older . . ."

She didn't have to finish her sentence, he knew exactly what she meant. If she had asked him three days before, he would have gotten up and left the room. But he had new memories of her now—the charming sight of her stuffing half a chocolate bar into her mouth like a little girl, the breathtaking sight of her above him, moonlight bathing her face, her head thrown back as she cried out in ecstasy. Going back to the way he had been with her was going to be nearly impossible. And he certainly couldn't do it tonight.

He exhaled a long breath. "When I first met you, you were an enchanting young girl on the verge of womanhood. You were always laughing, always smiling. A look from those dark eyes of yours could melt my heart. But I viewed you as my best friend's little sister. It was what worked for me. It was the way I kept you in perspective.

"Then one summer day after you had graduated from college, you came down to the police station where Nico and I were working. You were picking Nico up for lunch. You breezed into the station, beautiful, vivacious, bright, and alive. And it hit me. You were finally a woman.

"I had watched you grow more captivating, more lovely, with each passing year. That day you were bursting with spirit and fire, and you had your whole life before you. Something stirred in me that I had never felt before when I looked at you, but I had no trouble identifying the feeling. It was desire. I wanted to grab you to me, feel you against me, make love to you." She made a soft sound of surprise, and he smiled ruefully. "But I didn't, because at that moment I realized I was going to back away from you and stay away. I did exactly that, and I managed to sublimate my desire. I did it so well, I forgot it was even there."

"But why?" she said, blurting out the question.

"Because six years earlier, when I was on the police force in Texas, my wife had wandered into a dangerous situation and been killed. She was there because she had been out running errands, happened to see me, and came over. Intellectually I knew her death wasn't my fault. I even knew it had more to do with circumstances than it had to do with my job. But when I realized how much I wanted you that day, I also realized I had the same type of job as I had back then. The potential for danger was still there. I decided to give you the chance to live by staying away from you."

"Your reasoning doesn't make sense."

"Maybe it doesn't now. But on that particular day, at that particular moment, it made perfect sense to me."

"And now? You aren't working for the police department anymore. Your job's not dangerous, hasn't been for several years."

The sensual line of his lips firmed. "Habit is a powerful thing."

"So is what we shared the other night," she said daringly.

He looked at her. "What are you trying to do?"

"Understand, I guess."

He rolled his shoulders, an uneasiness in the movement. "It would be safer if we just forgot about it."

"Dammit." She bolted off the sofa in a flurry of silk violet, but he grabbed her wrist and pulled her back down against him.

His face was set in fierce lines and his eyes blazed. "Okay, you want an answer, I'll give you an answer. The minute Nico called me and asked me to look in on you, he gave me an excuse to seek you out that I would never have given myself. The problem is, once I had the excuse, my control started unraveling."

He released her arm, but she was too stunned by his outburst to move. She stayed where she was, her breasts pressed against the side of his arm.

"My father was a wildcatter. Time after time, he drilled, only to find a dry hole. My mother died when I was young and that left him and me. I can't tell you how many times the two of us had to pack up everything and move around West Texas until he found another spot he felt would be *the* place where he would hit a strike. He chose drinking to assuage his disappointment. By the time he did strike oil, he was too sick to enjoy it. But I learned early that if I maintained a level of control over myself and my emotions, the disappointment wouldn't get to me. My wife's death was a terrible blow to me. I loved her very much, but I forced myself to face my grief and anger over her death square on. I never allowed any of it to get the better of me, and I never lost the balanced sense of myself. I moved to Boston and made a new life. Then I met you." He paused. "I think all along I knew on some level deeper even than my subconscious that you would be the one to make me lose control. I was afraid of you. And that, Angelica, is why I stayed away from you."

"Me?" she whispered, shocked.

His gaze flicked to her lips. "I'm still afraid of you. Being with you completely goes against the grain of what I am. For years I managed to control my feelings for you when I wasn't even entirely conscious I had them. But now I've kissed you, made love to you, and I'm not sure I can find that kind of control again."

"Do you want to?"

"Yes."

She felt a stab of pain at his answer.

"I'm used to a life without you," he said, continuing. "It's a domain where nothing happens that I can't handle." He paused, staring at her, and his ferocity slowly faded to be replaced by an expression that was insidious and subversive in its heat. "And no, I don't want to. I've had a taste of what life would be like with you in it, and even though I can't seem to handle anything in that life where you and I are together, I'm not sure I can live any other way, at least for now."

She was overwhelmed. He had put at least a part of the puzzle together for her. What would happen next was up to her.

It was hard for her to believe he was afraid of her. A man like Amarillo wouldn't be afraid of many things. She also couldn't believe he could ever completely surrender his heart to a woman. He had said he couldn't imagine living any other kind of life—at least for now. He had given no promises, made no mention of love.

But it didn't matter, she realized.

She didn't question his honesty for a moment. He had opened himself up to her as much as he was able to, and if she wanted more, it was her problem.

At sixteen she had thought him wonderful and had had a crush on him. At twenty-seven she still thought him wonderful. But the crush had been replaced by love. She didn't know when it had happened. She didn't know why. She didn't even know how she felt abut it yet. She wasn't even shocked. Her world had stopped making sense, and for the time being she wasn't going to demand that it do so.

"Do you think the talk we just had could qualify as normal?" he asked, his gaze on her lips.

Her pulse was racing, she noticed absently. "Not by anyone's standards."

His long fingers framed her face. "Are you going to ask me to leave?"

"I don't have that kind of strength," she said, her voice hardly more than a breath.

His eyes darkened. "I couldn't have gone even if you'd asked me to."

He put his arms around her, lifted her from the couch, and carried her to the bed. He laid her down on the lace, then undressed. By the time he came down beside her, her violet chemise and robe lay in a puddle on the floor.

"Do you know what just occurred to me?" he asked unsteadily, running his hand over her breasts and down to her stomach.

She shook her head, finding a distinct thrill in the almost casual familiarity of lying naked beside him and in the commanding way he stroked her body. Even though they had been together for one whole night, it hadn't been like this. Then the lovemaking had been frantic and hungry. There was no doubt the hunger was *still* present, but now the urgency was submerged beneath a tantalizing tension. He wasn't hurrying, yet there was a tightly wound purpose and a special possessiveness about his touch that had a fire already burning in her belly.

"It just occurred to me that there might have been a reason why I missed your engagement party," he murmured huskily.

"I remember wondering where you were that night."

"I was sculling out on the river with a bottle of Jack Daniel's." His lips lightly fastened on the stiffened peak of her breast and pulled.

She gasped at the heat that coursed through her. And at the surprise she felt at his admission. "Why? My family was expecting you. *I* was expecting you."

He raised his head and stared down at the nipple. It seemed to him he saw a tiny bead of moisture pearled on its peak. He bent and licked it off, then licked again just because he couldn't resist. She made a small, sweet sound that tightened every muscle in his body. "At the time, I told myself I wasn't up to a party. A night's sculling on the river appealed to me much more. I don't know why I decided to take along the Jack Daniel's. I never had before or since."

He smoothed her dark hair back from her face and gazed down into her velvet-brown eyes. "When Nico picked me up for work the next morning, my head felt like Big Ben was inhabiting it. But when he told me you had backed out of the engagement at the last minute and asked your father not to make the announcement, I immediately felt better."

A soft smile of reminiscence touched her lips. "The whole reason for the party was to make the announcement. Roger had even given me the ring before the party began. But I looked around and suddenly something didn't seem right, something seemed missing. I gave the ring back."

"I'm glad," he said, a savage edge to his tone. "I'm glad he never had you. He wasn't good enough for you. Neither was Gary McKee." Compulsively he ran his hand over her again and felt her skin heat and soften beneath his touch.

"You didn't know Gary," she said breathlessly.

"I don't have to know him to know he wasn't good enough for you. No one is."

"Not even you?"

"Especially not me." He delved his fingers between her legs. "Do you like that?"

Her head went back, her neck arched off the pillow. *"Yes."*

The expression of ecstasy he saw on her face fired his mind and his body and made him close to crazy. Something inside him, something uncivilized and primitive, wanted him to be the only man who ever saw such a look on her face. "You know what I think?" he asked huskily, rising over her, the muscles of his arms rigid as he braced himself. "If I had known you were having an affair with him, I would have flown back from Texas and killed him." He entered her with such force that the lace on the canopy shimmied. He heard her gasp with pure pleasure and buried himself as deeply in her as he could.

A haze of heat closed around her. A feverish tension built and increased. She wrapped her legs around his wildly thrusting hips and gave herself up to the rapture that would come. And it was a long time until the lace stopped moving.

Sometime later he said, "Have you ever heard of a binary star system?"

"What?" she asked, uncertain if she had heard him right. She was half sprawled over him, her head resting on his chest, her dark hair streaming over him. And his voice was little more than a low purr in the darkness.

"A binary star system. It's a system of two stars that constantly revolve around each other under the influence of their mutual gravitation." He wove his fingers through her hair, then closed his hand around a silky fistful. "They are both bright, both burning, and they can't break away from each other. It's like a compulsion; they have to keep circling. I think you and I, without being aware of it, have, for many years, formed our own binary star system."

She lifted her head and stared down at him. "That's a very poetic thing to say."

"I'm not poetic."

"You compared us to two bright and burning stars who aren't able to break away from each other. That's poetic."

"That's scientific."

"It's a beautiful analogy."

"It's a truthful analogy."

She grinned. "You just won't give at all, will you?"

He returned her grin. "Nope."

She rested her head on his chest again and listened to his steady heartbeat. The room was illuminated by moonlight and firelight. The French door that opened onto the terrace stood ajar. Air entered and drifted across the room to beneath the lace canopy, cooling their bodies.

Angelica felt satisfied and complete in a way she had never known existed. Yet something she couldn't identify was bothering her.

She had admitted to herself that she was in love with Amarillo. He had admitted that, for now, he couldn't do without her. She should be able to give herself up to the happiness of the moment. Why couldn't she, she asked herself as she felt Amarillo's arms tighten around her.

He rolled her over and slowly entered her. Once again heat engulfed her, obliterating thought—and stilling the inner voice that was telling her something was very wrong.

Six

The ringing of the phone woke Angelica. Beside her, she felt Amarillo stir.

"Do you want me to answer it?" he murmured.

"No, I'll get it." As she stretched to reach for the phone, she squinted at the clock. "Heavens, it's not even six o'clock yet. Who on earth—hello?"

"Hi," Nico said on the other end of the line. "What are you doing?"

"Sleeping."

"Well, wake up and talk to me."

"Why?" She turned her head and mouthed *Nico* to Amarillo. He made a face.

"Because I want to talk to you. It's a great day here in beautiful downtown Rome. We've been out sight-seeing and spending money. We came back to the hotel for a little while, to rest, refuel, restock Dev's diaper bag, that sort of thing. I thought while we were here, I would check in with you."

LET YOURSELF BE LOVESWEPT BY... SIX BRAND NEW LOVESWEPT ROMANCES!

Because Loveswept romances sell themselves ...we want to send you six (Yes, six!) exciting new novels to enjoy for 15 days — risk free! — without obligation to buy.

Discover how these compelling stories of contemporary romances tug at your heart strings and keep you turning the pages. Meet true-to-life characters you'll fall in love with as their romances blossom. Experience their challenges and triumphs — their laughter, tears and passion.

Let yourself be Loveswept! Join our **at-home reader service!** Each month we'll send you six new Loveswept novels **before they appear in the bookstores.** Take up to **15 days to preview** current selections **risk-free! Keep only those shipments you want.** Each book is yours for only $2.09 plus postage & handling, and sales tax where applicable — **a savings of 41¢ per book** off the cover price.

NO OBLIGATION TO BUY — WITH THIS RISK-FREE OFFER!

YOU GET SIX ROMANCES RISK FREE...
Plus AN EXCLUSIVE TITLE FREE!

Loveswept Romances

AFFIX
RISK FREE
BOOKS
STAMP
HERE.

Kay Hooper's
**Larger
Than
Life**

This FREE gift
is yours to keep.

MY "NO RISK" GUARANTEE

There's no obligation to buy and the free gift is mine to keep. I may preview each subsequent shipment for 15 days. If I don't want it, I simply return the books within 15 days and owe nothing. If I keep them, I will pay just $2.09 per book. I save $2.50 off the retail price for the 6 books (plus postage and handling, and sales tax where applicable).

YES! Please send my six Loveswept novels
RISK FREE along with my **FREE GIFT**
described inside the heart!   **BR78**   10124

NAME_____

ADDRESS_____ APT_____

CITY_____

STATE_____ ZIP_____

Amarillo curved his arm around her waist and drew her back against the hard contours of his body. Instantly heat flooded through her. *Even* at six o'clock in the morning, *even* after a night of lovemaking. Her mouth twisted wryly. What was she going to do about this tendency of hers to react so absurdly to him?

"Angelica?"

"I'm here. I was just thinking that somehow I don't believe you've quite gotten the knack of vacationing yet. You're checking in entirely too often."

"That's what Caitlin says."

"She's right."

"That remains to be seen. At any rate, I spoke with your office late yesterday and they told me you'd be at SwanSea. How is it?"

"It hasn't changed."

"I *meant* how are things going, Angelica? Has anyone ever told you that you're not at your best conversationally at six A.M.?"

"Now that you know—"

"I also called *my* office yesterday. They told me Rill's there too. Have you seen him?"

Now, how did she answer that? *Yes, he's right here in the bed beside me. We just spent a fabulous night making love.* "If you want to know whether he checked up on me the other day as you asked him to, then the answer is yes."

"I know. He left a message at the hotel the next day. But have you seen him since?"

Her brother was nothing if not persistent. "Is there something you want me to tell him if I do?"

"Yeah, tell him hi. Tell him—oh, here, Caitlin wants to speak with you."

"No," she said quickly. "I'll speak with her later—"

"Angelica?"

Amarillo nuzzled her neck. She loved her brother and his wife dearly, she reflected ruefully, but talking to them this early in the morning when Amarillo had suddenly become engrossed in finding every sensitive spot that existed on her neck, shoulder, and ear ranked at the bottom of the list regarding things she wanted to do. With an effort she checked her impatience. "Hi, Caitlin."

"Sorry to call so early. I tried to tell him."

"That's all right, but next time he gets the urge to call, hit him in the head with something."

"I will. In fact, I bought a marble urn today that will work beautifully. I'm having a great time shopping. Wait until you see everything I've bought. But anyway, what I really wanted to talk about was the preparations for the ball. How are they coming along?"

"Just fine. We're down to the wire now and things will be stepping up."

"I'd say I wish I were there helping you, but I wouldn't mean it. We're having too much fun. And I'm glad we brought Dev with us. I know he's too young to know where he is and what he's seeing, and it's a real hassle carting around all his baby paraphernalia, but if we had left him at home with a nurse, I would be spending all my time worrying about him."

"Worrying about him?" She smiled as Amarillo's teeth fastened onto her earlobe and chewed lightly.

"I'm afraid so. We have the best staff and security system in the world, but I would still worry about his safety. I guess that's normal though."

Unaccountably Angelica felt herself tense. "His safety?"

"I worry about everything from a scrape on his knee to a kidnapping. No one told me that worrying so much was in a mother's job description."

"Kidnapping? Have you had any threats?"

"Good heavens, no! Paranoia is a condition all mothers have, believe me. Just you wait. One day you'll have it too. Listen, I'd better go. Tell Rill hi when you see him, and don't work too hard. The ball will happen with or without perfection on your part. The main thing is to relax and have fun. See you soon. 'Bye."

"Good-bye." She replaced the receiver and gazed up at the underside of the lace canopy.

"What's wrong?" Amarillo asked.

"Nothing. I'm supposed to relax and have fun."

"Good advice, but what was that about threats?"

"Threats? Oh, Caitlin was just telling me that she's glad they decided to take Dev with them. Otherwise she would be spending all her time worrying about him."

He chuckled. "I don't know why. Nico and I designed their security system ourselves. A fly couldn't get into their house without the authorities being notified." He touched a finger to her wrinkled brow. "What's this? Did she say something to upset you?"

"No, of course not. It's just that I guess I've

never considered the possibility that little Dev might get kidnapped. It's a frightening thought."

"Yes, it is, but Dev is as safe as any child can be, so don't worry."

"You're right." She exhaled, deliberately releasing her tension with her breath. "By the way, they both said hi to you."

"It's always nice to be remembered." He dropped a kiss on her smooth shoulder. "Why didn't you tell them I was here with you? Are you afraid they would be shocked or disapprove?"

"No, no. As a matter of fact, Nico would probably be delighted that his best friend and his sister were together." Whether he would like the way their relationship would eventually end remained to be seen, she reflected. For her too.

She came up on one elbow so that she could see him better. His body was angled toward her; the lace-edged white sheet draped over the jut of his hips and down his abdomen to below his navel. Light-colored hair covered his bronze chest. She skimmed her fingers through the thickness, thinking with wonder that she loved this man. And for the time being, at least, she had him all to herself. "You know what?"

He grinned lazily up at her. "No, what?"

"Most men would look silly lying amid all this lace, but you look even more masculine. How do you do it?"

"I haven't the slightest idea what you're talking about."

"The lace. You should be uncomfortable, out of place. After all, you look like you were formed out of West Texas bedrock."

His grin widened. "How do you know what West Texas bedrock looks like?"

"It looks like you. Magnificent. Hard. There's no softness anywhere in you."

"Oh, Angelica." He pulled her back down and kissed her. "That's not true. There's a lot of softness in me—at least for you." He grinned. "Much more than is good for me probably."

"I don't know if I believe that."

"I'll prove it to you. We'll do anything you want today. What do you want to do? Horseback ride? Swim? Tennis? The beach?"

She shook her head regretfully. "I've got to work today. The ball," she added by way of explanation. "I have a whole list of people I need to see, things I have to do."

"You're not going to work," he said firmly.

She grinned. "I thought you said you'd do what *I* wanted."

"I will. The thing is, you don't really want to work."

"I don't?"

"No," he said with a twinkle in his golden eyes that made him all the more irresistible to her. "You want to play with me."

"Play? You've never struck me as a man who plays." As soon as she spoke, she remembered the electric train set in his warehouse home. She started to mention it, but he pulled her closer and buried his face in her hair.

"Occasionally I play. Occasionally, with women who have velvet-brown eyes and silky brown hair."

"And do you find many women who have these particular qualities?"

"Not a lot."

"That's good. That's real good."

"It's still early," he murmured. "Do you feel like going back to sleep?" he asked.

"No."

"Do you want to get up and take a shower with me?"

A delicious warmth spread through her at the thought. "I'll have to think about it. What other options are open to me?"

"Stay here in bed with me . . . and play."

She tilted her head back. "I have an idea. Why don't I stay here in bed with you . . . and play. Then, later, get up and take a shower with you."

"What great ideas," he said, and took possession of her mouth.

The sun was setting as Amarillo and Angelica walked through the front doors of SwanSea and into the great hall.

She laughed breathlessly up at him. "Admit it, croquet is a game of finesse and skill."

His lips quirked, enjoying her mirthful mood. "Where's the finesse and skill? You hit a ball through a wire hoop. Big deal."

"Oh, yeah? Then why did I beat you?"

"I was distracted."

"By what?" she asked, clearly skeptical.

"By that pretty behind of yours. Every time you bent over to hit the ball. You have no idea the thoughts that went through my head. Did you have those jeans especially made to fit you?"

"No, I bought them right off the shelf. Quit making excuses."

"Excuses? You've obviously never seen that fantastic bottom of yours from my perspective or you'd understand. But you know what? I'm willing to forget and forgive if, once we're upstairs, you could demonstrate some of your croquet techniques to me, you know, under more controlled conditions. You could bend over and I could—"

She laughed and hit his chest. "You are *so* bad!"

"That's not a no, is it?"

"Miss DiFrenza?"

Still laughing, she turned to find Peter. "Hi."

He nodded and handed her a thick stack of messages and mail. "These have come in for you today while you've been out."

She grimaced. "Thanks. I guess this is what I get for playing hooky." She glanced up at Amarillo. "Tomorrow, I work."

"Maybe."

"Definitely."

"Maybe," he said again, while his eyes twinkled in the way she found so irresistible.

"These are your messages, Mr. Smith," Peter said, handing Amarillo a lesser stack.

"Thanks." He paused to sift through them, then turned to Angelica. "Listen, I need to get back to a couple of these people right away. Why don't I go to my room and make the calls, shower, and change, then meet you in your room in about fifteen minutes. We can discuss dinner."

She stood on tiptoe and kissed him. "And maybe even the finer points of croquet."

Amarillo strode down the fourth floor hall toward Angelica's room. It had been only a little while since they had parted, but he was impatient and eager to see her again. It amazed him.

He was used to being alone. He *liked* being alone. But more and more he was finding that when she was away from him, both his mind and his senses felt absolute emptiness.

He halted in front of her door, raised his hand to knock, but then on a hunch gripped the door-knob, turned it, and opened the door.

Angelica was sitting on the floor in front of the fireplace, her head tilted toward the fire so that the heat could better reach her wet hair. She was wearing the short violet robe, he noted, and, his male instinct told him, nothing else.

At the sound of the door closing, she looked around, saw him, and smiled. "Hi. Did you get your calls made?"

"Why wasn't this door locked?"

Her smile of greeting changed to one of amusement. "I'll go out on a limb and say it wasn't locked because I didn't lock it."

He crossed the room to her, reached down for her outstretched hand, and helped her to her feet. "Keep the door locked, Angelica."

"Why? You and I are the only two staying up here on the fourth floor. The staff doesn't come onto the floor unless we call for them. The other guests can't get on this floor either by stairs or elevator."

"That's not the point—"

She playfully tugged at the collar of his shirt. "Do you realize we could play hide-and-seek in the nude and no one would see us?" Her eyes took on a mischievous light. "And now that I think about it, that's a terrific idea!"

Faced with her good mood and her sexy attire, he couldn't remain stern. "It's a great idea," he agreed, dropping onto the sofa and drawing her down beside him. "Except why don't we change th rules a little. Instead of one of us hiding and the other seeking, why don't we hide together."

Her eyes widened with mock innocence. "But then there wouldn't be anyone to seek."

He wrapped a still-damp strand of her dark brown hair around his finger and used it to pull her gently toward him. He kissed her lightly, then murmured, "Yeah, but who would care?"

She grinned. "Good point."

He straightened away from her. "Thank you. And I have another good point. From now on, lock the door."

"You're like a dog with a bone, aren't you? You just won't stop until you get your way."

His lips twitched with humor. "A dog with a bone, Angelica? My, my, that's a very un-socialite turn of phrase. Where did you learn it?"

"I have no idea. Probably from my brother, who probably learned it from you. Now, answer my original question. Did you get your calls made? Do we have a free evening ahead of us?"

He nodded. "I did, and in answer to your second question, as far as I'm concerned we do. What about you?"

She glanced over at an end table, where she'd dumped her messages and mail on the way into the bathroom to take a shower. "I'm sure there's nothing I can't leave until tomorrow. I hope so, anyway, because that's my plan." She idly reached for a letter and slit it open with a manicured nail. "What would you like to do? Shall we dress and go downstairs for dinner?"

"I don't know. Since it's obvious you'd rather put off my idea of croquet demonstrations under controlled conditions for a while—"

She grinned. "Just for a while. Not for long. I can see how much it means to you."

"Uh-huh. Well, until you get into another croquet state of mind, I kind of liked your idea about hide-and-seek, using my rules of course. We hide together and *pretend* there's someone after us. That way, we can maintain the suspense of the game, plus have each other to share the fun."

"What about my rule of no clothes?"

He nodded. "It's a good rule. I say we keep it."

"You know, I had no idea you were such a game-playing sort of person."

"I told you, only with women who have velvet-brown eyes and silky brown hair."

She grinned, pulled the letter from the envelope, and scanned it. "A last-minute plea for tickets." She handed him the letter and reached for another envelope. "I'll have to tell them that they're welcome to come to the ball," she said, opening the next envelope, "but unfortunately they won't be able to stay here. I'm happy to say SwanSea is booked to capacity for the weekend."

He recognized the name on the letter. "It won't be any trouble for them to fly their private jet in for the evening. Mr. Lawrence can send a car to the airport for them." He glanced at her and saw her pulling out a letter from the second envelope. "Hey, I thought you were going to wait until tomorrow."

"I am, but they're kind of like potato chips, I can't seem to open just one. I promise, though, this will be the last." She bent her head to the letter, and in the next moment felt the blood drain from her face.

Amarillo saw her go pale. "What's wrong?"

Without saying a word, she handed him the sheet of paper.

He looked down and saw that letters had been cut from magazines and pasted together to form a message. It read:

Come back home now! If you don't start minding me, I'll make you mind me.

"Dammit!" He grabbed up the envelope and saw that it was addressed to her at SwanSea and had been postmarked from Boston. "The bastard changed his method of operating. I put a trace on your phone here, but I didn't think to intercept your mail."

Her glance shot to the phone by her bed, then back to him. "You put a trace on my phone without telling me?"

"You bet I did, and I offer no apology."

She was too shaken by the note to argue with him. She took the sheet of paper back from him and stared down at the pasted letters. "I thought I had left this behind in Boston."

"I was hoping he wouldn't be smart enough to put two and two together immediately and realize you were here."

"But you said that no one followed me."

"No one did. Unfortunately this guy is tenacious, and on top of that he seems to know a lot about you."

Her eyes widened with horror. "Do you mean this person might be an acquaintance of mine?"

"I don't have enough to go on yet to say for certain, but it's possible. Or he could be a stranger who has made you his obsession and has studied you to the point that he knows everything a person can who is outside your family and circle of friends."

"You're frightening me."

He had chosen his words for that very effect. As much as he hated the apprehension he saw in her eyes, he had felt it necessary to be blunt with her. "You didn't take the phone calls seriously. I hope now you'll understand why I think you should take precautions."

"What sort of precautions?"

"You need to be under guard."

She shot off the couch and circled around behind it. "Absolutely not!"

He turned so he could see her. "Angelica, didn't you read the note? He said if you didn't mind him, he would make you mind him. That's a *threat.* He's saying, in effect, that if you don't do as he says and go home, he will do something to make you."

A wave of panic rose up in her. She waited until it had receded before she went on. "He's only using words, Amarillo. Letters pasted on a page. He hasn't actually done anything harmful to me."

"Not yet."

She propped a hip on the back of the couch. "Look, I don't have a death wish or any other kind of awful wish for that matter. I will take reasonable precautions, but *I* will define the term *reasonable*."

"Oh, hell, Angelica, who are you trying to impress? I know your definition of reasonable. You'll lock the door when you remember to, and you'll allow me to continue the phone tap without too much grumbling, and that's about it."

"The man is in Boston, Amarillo!"

"How do you know? He could have mailed this to you on his way out of town. He could be here by now."

"Here at SwanSea?" She shook her head. "No."

He reached up, grabbed her wrist, and with a tug pulled her down to him and positioned her so she lay across his lap and her head was in the crook of his arm. "We have to talk about this, Angelica. Now."

She smiled faintly; the heat had already begun to grow in her as soon as her body had come into contact with his. "And that's why you pulled me down here?"

"I want your complete attention."

"You have it, believe me."

"Okay, tell me, can you think of anyone who might be doing this to you?"

Her smile faded. "It can't be anyone I know."

"We have to consider the possibility."

She sat up, abruptly stripping herself from his arms. "No, no! I tell you, it's no one I know."

He pulled her back down to where she had been. He smoothed away the hair from her face, not because her hair needed attention, but more because he felt better touching her. And as long as he was holding her, he could trick himself into feeling more in control. "It's a horrible thought, I know. For a while you were able to convince yourself that he was just some jerk who would eventually go away. By doing that, you were able to feel safe. But in this case, feeling safe is dangerous."

She gazed up at him, her expression now completely solemn. "How can you be so sure this is going to turn into something more than mild harassment?"

"It's a gut feeling."

"Nico used to say he could take your gut feelings to the bank."

A crease deepened in one cheek. "It's you I've got to convince."

She exhaled a long breath. "The answer to your question is no, I don't know anyone who would want to call me and say those strange things or send me the note."

"Okay, then, let's go at this another way. Instead of looking at who could have sent you the note, let's look at *why*. The note said, 'Come back home now.' So why would someone want you to go back home? What's there?"

"Him? He's probably still there."

"Maybe." He gazed thoughtfully down at her. "Coming at it from another angle, we could ask, what's here that he doesn't want you involved with?"

"Well, it's not you, because the calls started the night before you came to see me at the office."

He nodded. "That pretty much leaves the ball."

"The ball?"

"The ball is the reason you're here. Didn't he say during one of his calls that you should be a good girl and stay home?"

"Something like that. Seems like he definitely wanted me to stay back in Boston." She grimaced. "But you're off the mark with the ball. For heaven's sake, it's for the Children's Fund. Nothing could be more harmless or, I might add, more worthwhile."

"When you have nothing to go on, Angelica, all theories are fair for consideration."

"I suppose."

"I'm going to run a check on all the guests." She stiffened, but he was prepared for her displeasure with his decision. "Don't worry, I will be ultra discreet. No one will know. No one will be offended. Trust me."

She rested her head against his shoulder, seeking comfort and warmth, and thought about his request to trust him. He was the kind of man who inspired confidence in others, and there was no doubt in her mind that she could trust him with her safety, and if it came down to it, her life.

Trusting him with her heart was another matter. Her love for him was too new, too fragile to expose. With each moment she spent with him, her feelings of love for him were growing stronger, larger. He was rapidly becoming everything to her, but she understood that his emotions weren't so deeply involved.

She trusted him not to deliberately hurt her, and in a relationship such as theirs, where only she loved, that was all she could reasonably ask. Above all, she had to remember a hugely important fact—he hadn't asked her to trust him with her heart. Only her safety.

Her robe had come undone; she looked up and saw that his eyes had darkened with yearning. Until that moment she hadn't realized she was wanting him too, but it was there—the passion, the desire, the need. She wrapped her arms around his neck and drew his mouth down to hers.

He made love slowly to her on the floor in front of the fire. With his touches he created a burning that became a seemingly permanent part of her skin, with his kisses he ignited a raging inferno inside her that not only lasted but built.

She had a craving for him—for the feel of him, the smell of him, the weight of him on top of her. He seemed to sense her neediness and responded with a generosity that took her breath away. He gave to her until tears clung to her lashes and she was crying out his name. He gave to her until she couldn't take any more. He gave to her until he was crying out her name.

Angelica was frightened, terribly frightened. Somewhere a child was whimpering, somewhere there was the sound of music and laughter. She caught a scent of English lavender, and she heard the familiar, sweet voice say, "She shouldn't be going out. She should stay home on a night like this. It's too cold." Then, "Be good. Be good."

The voice faded. Another voice, one she hadn't heard before, one that was deeper, gruffer, spoke to her. Rough hands grabbed her, and she started to cry.

"Mind me, dammit!" the man said. "If you don't mind me, I'll *make* you mind me!"

She tried to stop crying, but she couldn't. The orchestra was playing dance music. Then it was dark and she was so cold. The silence she heard terrified her. She screamed and screamed but no one heard her.

Her first scream woke Amarillo. "Angelica? Good Lord!"

He jerked upright, switched on the bedside light, then quickly turned to her. And his heart almost failed at what he saw. She was twisting and thrashing as if she were trying to fend off some enemy only she could see. Sweat covered her body and plastered her dark hair to her head. Worst of all, her face was contorted with sheer terror.

"Angelica, what's wrong? Honey, wake up and tell me what's wrong."

He grasped her shoulders and lightly shook her, but she struck out at him with balled-up fists.

"Angelica sweetheart, wake up. It's Amarillo. You're safe. You're just having a nightmare." He saw the tears streaming down her cheeks and cursed. The nightmare had her in a terrible grip and he couldn't free her.

She felt someone gently stroking her brow. The music had faded; Amarillo's voice filled the silence. Where was he, she wondered, sobbing. If only she could find him. If only someone would find her.

In desperation, Amarillo yanked a blanket from the bottom of the bed, wrapped her in it, then carried her across the room to a chair that sat in front of the low-burning fire. He settled into it, held her close against him, and rocked her.

He pressed his mouth to her forehead. "Shhh, sweetheart, don't cry, please don't cry. Wake up now, wake up. Everything's all right."

His big body warmed her, his low, soft purring voice soothed her. Somehow she realized he was holding her. Little by little the fear receded until slowly she lifted her eyelids and looked up at him.

Relief beyond measure flooded through him. He smoothed a shaky hand across her brow, brushing damp strands of hair away from her face. "There now," he said softly. "See? You're awake and you're safe. It was only a dream."

"Yes." She felt as if he had rescued her from something terrible, unendurable. She just didn't know what it could have been.

"That was some dream you were having," he murmured, aware that he was still rocking her, still stroking her, but unable to stop. And he didn't know if he was doing it for him or for her. "What was it about?"

"I don't know. It didn't make sense."

She sounded like a frightened little girl, and he was overwhelmed by the urge to slay dragons for her. "Dreams are that way most of the time. It's hard to tell what they mean and why they come to you. But in this case, the dream could have been triggered by the note you received earlier. Goodness knows, it was enough to upset anyone." He pressed a kiss to her forehead. "Forget the dream. It's gone now."

She was sure he was right. She had been understandably disturbed over the note. It had said, "If you don't mind me, I'll make you mind me." Someone had said the same thing to her in her dream, someone she was afraid of. It made sense.

So why then did she think the explanation for her dream was more complicated than that? And why was she afraid of finding out the answer?

"Do you want to go back to bed now?" he asked.

"No. Can we just stay here for a while?"

He gathered her closer to him. "As long as you like."

Seven

Winston Lawrence caught sight of Angelica coming down the grand staircase and went to meet her. "Miss DiFrenza, a phone call for you has been mistakenly put through to the front desk. I was about to take a message, but since you're here, would you like to go ahead and accept it?"

Angelica's step faltered, and she came to a stop at the bottom of the staircase. "Did the caller give a name?"

"Oh, yes, I'm sorry I didn't mention it before. It's a Mr. William Breckinridge of DiFrenza's."

Her sigh of relief was almost audible. After last night's dream and its traumatic aftermath, she wasn't up to facing another strange phone call. She crossed the great hall to the phone. "Hello, Mr. Breckinridge. How are things going?"

"Highly satisfactory, Miss DiFrenza, which is one of the reasons I'm calling. I wanted to assure you that I have everything under control. Eleven sets of jewels have been chosen. They're all packed and ready for me to bring."

"Have you had to referee any disagreements among the ladies, two of them wanting the same necklace?"

"I'm happy to report that this year, unlike several in the past, everything has gone quite smoothly."

"And what about the rubies? Have you had a chance to go to the bank yet?"

There was a pause. "Not as yet. I suppose the bank will be one of the last things I do before I leave for SwanSea, that is if you haven't changed your mind about the Deverell rubies."

"I won't. I'm looking forward to wearing them. In fact, I can hardly wait."

"I take it, then, that your ballgown has been completed."

"Yes, I have it here with me." She glanced down at the list in her hand, then at her watch. She had an appointment to see the chef in five minutes. "When will you be arriving, Mr. Breckinridge?"

"If the schedule stays the same, day after tomorrow."

"Fine, fine. I'll see you then. Good-bye." She hung up the phone, took another look at the list, and realized she had left off the head gardener of the greenhouse. Damn. Well, she would just have to squeeze him in.

"So this is where you are," Amarillo said to Angelica, strolling into the ballroom later that day. "I've been looking for you."

She was sitting on the floor beside the center chandelier that had been lowered for cleaning. It was a giant exotic flower made up of sparkling crystal petals. At the sound of his voice she looked around at him with a smile. "I'm surprised you found me. I didn't think anyone would look for me in here."

He dropped down to the sun-warmed floor beside her. "Were you trying to hide?"

"Just looking for a moment's peace. I've had nonstop appointments all day."

He nodded and propped his arm on a raised knee. "I'm glad to hear you weren't trying to avoid me."

She laughed. "Somehow I don't think I would have much luck in hiding from you if you were really trying to find me."

He grinned. "You're right about that. I have two things going for me. One, I'm a detective. And two, I never give up. Oh, and there is a third thing."

"What's that?"

"You pull me to you, just like a magnet."

Her smile softened, and he leaned toward her, intending to kiss her, but he hit his head on the chandelier. The crystals shimmied and tinkled one against the other. And color shot from their prism centers, causing fairylike rainbow designs to dance over her.

"Look at the rainbows," she exclaimed, laughing. "Aren't they pretty?"

"Pretty, but I'd rather look at you. I can't reach out and touch a rainbow, there'd be nothing there." He ran a finger down the side of her throat. "But I can touch you."

She heated all over. "Yes, you can. Anytime, anyplace."

He felt himself begin to grow hard. *Damn.* He wanted her all the time now. This compulsive desire for her was growing, not diminishing—and it spoke of dependency. Better to get his mind on another subject. He glanced around, taking in the gold, silver, and crystal room. "Why did you choose this place as a hideout?"

"I don't know. I've always liked it here. Caitlin once told me that her grandmother, Arabella, felt the same way. You'd think a room as enormous as this would be cold, but it's not. It's a warm, happy room. I've always thought I'd like to attend a ball here."

"I'm not surprised. You love parties, the larger the better."

"That's not true," she said quickly, suppressing a sudden shudder. "As a matter of fact, I've *never* liked balls or galas. There something about them that makes me very uncomfortable."

He frowned. "Now, I'm surprised. You're always the life of any party."

She moved her shoulders, uncomfortable about explaining something she'd never really understood herself. "I've always dreaded large parties, but if my family is there, I feel better about it. And once I get there and I see people I know, I'm usually okay."

"I would think *okay* is an understatement. Honey, I've seen you positively sizzle."

She grinned. "You were paying attention?"

"There were times I couldn't take my eyes off you."

"You know what? Sometimes I had the same problem with you."

He nodded slowly. "It's only fair."

Her grin widened. "Would you like to hear my theory about rooms and houses?"

"If you have a theory," he said solemnly, "then I have an obligation to hear it."

She noted the twinkle in his eye and punched him lightly in the arm. "Okay, here it is. I think houses absorb and store up the things that happen inside them, I think that's what gives them their character and personality."

Amarillo cleared his throat. "That's an interesting theory, all right. Do we have any scientists working on it at the moment?"

She sent him a look meant to quell, but that succeeded only in increasing the twinkle in his eye. "Okay, now, take this room for instance. It's known parties and dances galore. It's even had at least one wedding that we know of held in it. Remember? Nico and Caitlin were married here."

"I remember. You wore violet."

She grimaced. "Violet, of course." She shook her head. "I'm beginning to believe that I have a very weird mind."

He grinned. "Luckily, I get very turned on by weird."

She laughed, and the sound traveled through the empty room, then came back to her as a faint echo. She looked at him. "See what I mean? It's a happy room."

He reached out and touched her. "I don't know

about the room," he said quietly, "but I'm glad to see you happy."

She decided not to let him know how fleeting she felt this happiness was. He would want to know why, she wouldn't be able to explain, and they would both get upset. "Remember Elena here on Nico and Caitlin's wedding day? Now, *there* was someone who was happy."

He nodded in agreement. "She glowed. It was wonderful that she could come to SwanSea at least once before she died."

"And that she lived to see her family united with her husband's family. It gave her such peace in her last year. I'm very grateful for it. Caitlin told her what she had heard of that time after Elena's husband John was killed in the war. According to lore passed down among SwanSea servants, Edward closed himself up in his rooms and didn't come out until months later. The servants put the mail aside and eventually bundled it up into the attic. Edward never received Elena's Bible or letter. He never knew he had a daughter-in-law or a grandson. If he had known, I'm sure Deverell history would have been rewritten." Angelica shrugged her shoulders.

He pushed a heavy strand of her hair away from her face. "You might have grown up right here at SwanSea. Have you ever thought about that?"

"No, but I've never felt deprived. It hasn't been that many years since I learned I was a Deverell. The news was a wonderful, astonishing surprise, but nothing can take away from the DiFrenza part of me. Thanks to Elena, I already had a complete and rich life and heritage. Knowing about the Deverells' connection to us and about SwanSea is simply an enrichment of that life and heritage."

"What a nice way to look at it."

"The first time I saw SwanSea, I had the strangest sensation of coming home. It was as if this place had always been waiting for me. I love coming here to visit, but I wouldn't change anything about my life up until now. I don't feel as if I've lost anything. I feel as if I've gained." Especially her time with him, she thought. She reached out and caressed his face, and it occurred to her that this was a very precious moment, talking quietly with him in the surrounding warmth and sunshine of the room.

He took her hand, kissed its palm, then curled his hand around hers. "Your mother died when you were very young, didn't she?"

"I was about two and a half years old. If I didn't have photographs of her, I wouldn't remember her at all. Elena became my mother. If I hadn't had her—"

Amarillo suddenly frowned. "Are we making you sad by talking about your mother and Elena?"

She laughed at him in surprise. "No. Why?"

"I don't know. Just a feeling I got."

He was very perceptive, she thought. He had realized before she had that her spirits were falling. He had the reason wrong, though. It wasn't what they were talking about that was the cause, but rather her growing belief that a peaceful, quiet time with him like this might not happen again.

There was a darkness threatening her, and she was frightened. She didn't know from where the darkness was coming, but she was certain it would eventually entomb her. A strange sort of cold sensation gripped her, chilling her to the bone. She glanced around the beautiful, sun-filled room, then back to him. She could still feel the room's warmth, and she knew he could make her feel heat.

She reached for him. "Make love to me."

"Here? Now?"

"No one will come in."

"How do you know?"

"Please," she whispered, her lips against his.

He shouldn't, he thought. At least not until he had locked or barred the doors in some way. But he was only human, a man obsessed with one woman, *this* woman. And there was an urgency in her. He could no more turn down her request to make love than he could fly.

To be able to touch her was a guarantee that his heart would beat one more time. To be able to slide into her and feel her close tightly around him was insurance that he would continue to breathe. Without these things he might die.

He helped her undress, then undressed himself.

He touched her, he slid into her; he continued to live.

Currents of air drifted around the huge room, brushing over the crystals of the chandeliers. Sweet, clear, bell-like music sounded, and rainbows of color played over their skin. And their happiness and pleasure in each other seemed to saturate the ballroom and be absorbed into its very walls.

* * *

Angelica was frightened. She couldn't see; everything was dark, black. She heard a child crying. The child was so scared, so bewildered, she didn't understand the muted voices outside. But they grew louder, angrier.

"Stupid woman! You're worrying about the wrong things."

"Don't be angry with me. I love you. You're my golden-haired boy. It hurts me when you call me names."

"Then do what I say, *exactly* what I say."

"I will. I love you."

The door was jerked open. The dark silhouette of a man appeared against a dim light. "Look at her. She's filthy! And she's always crying. I told her if she doesn't start minding me, she'll be sorry, because I'll *make* her mind me."

"She needs to go home."

"She will, if she minds me, and if you do as I say."

The man grabbed her and scrubbed her face hard with a rough cloth that scraped her skin. It hurt so bad; every time he touched her he hurt her. She cried and cried. He slapped her, knocking her backward onto the old mattress, and then there was darkness again. And she was all alone. All alone.

Angelica came wide awake and sat straight up in bed, gasping for air. Arms reached out for her. *"No!"* She hit the arms away and scrambled for the end of the bed.

Nico's hands closed around her upper arms,

holding her back. "What's wrong, sweetheart? Where are you going? Did you have another dream?"

She swung wildly around, dislodging his grip on her. "Don't *touch* me!"

"All right," he said, his tone calm and soothing. "All right. Just let me switch on a light." He leaned over, clicked on the bedside lamp, then turned to look at her, and his heart leapt into his throat. She was kneeling at the end of the bed, hunched, ready to bolt. Her face was pale, her eyes were wide and filled with fear; beneath the violet chemise her chest rose and fell with agitation. She looked like some wild, helpless creature who was being hunted, he thought with anguish. "Did you have another dream?" he whispered, careful not to make an unexpected move.

"Dream?" She didn't know. She couldn't explain what had just gone on in her mind, and most of all, she was afraid to try. "No."

"Then what's wrong?"

"Nothing. Leave me alone."

"I'm not touching you, Angelica. Come back up here beside me. Get under the covers. I don't want you to get chilled."

She tilted her head, listening. His voice was low, quiet, a soft, velvet purr, so unlike those she had just heard in her mind. *She had heard those voices before.* Who were those people? The man had said she was filthy. The woman had called him her golden-haired boy. Her glance flew to Amarillo. His hair was sandy-colored. And he was looking at her with concern.

She put a hand to her face where the man had slapped her. She could still feel the stinging hurt.

"I've got to wash." She scrambled off the bed and hurried into the bathroom. The lights were blindingly bright at first, but she didn't care. She grabbed a washcloth, wet and soaped it, then began to scrub her face. She pushed the cloth hard back and forth over her cheeks. It was painful, but she couldn't stop. The man had called her filthy. She rinsed the cloth with hot, steaming water and started the process again.

Amarillo came up behind her and lightly put his hands on her shoulders. Fear instantly seized her. She pushed back against him, trying for maneuvering room so that she could get free of him.

"Don't fight me, honey. I'm not going to hurt you." He wrapped one arm around her, and with the other reached to pry the cloth away from her.

She turned and hit out at him. "Give that back to me! I need it!"

He tossed the cloth across the room, grabbed her wrists, and held them to his chest. "You're going to injure yourself, Angelica."

"Don't be silly. I'm just washing."

He cupped his hand along the side of her cheek and flicked his thumb back and forth across the reddened skin. "There's not a speck of dirt on you, sweetheart."

Tears welled in her eyes, and her voice broke. "There must be."

He had never felt so powerless in his life. She was going through something awful, and he didn't know how to help her. He slowly shook his head and swept her up into his arms. "Come on, let me take you back to bed."

The thought of going back to bed, the place where she had had the dream, terrified her, and she began to struggle, pushing against his chest. "No, I don't want to be in bed!"

He stopped and gazed down at her. The fear was still there in her eyes, as were the tears. He wanted to curse, to vent this terrible anger he felt because she was so upset and it seemed nothing he could do or say made any difference. Instead, he asked very gently, "Where do you want to be?"

"Anyplace but the bed."

He carried her to the sofa, and after laying her down he bent to the fireplace and built a fire. Then he returned to the bed and scooped up a blanket, but when he leaned toward the lamp on the bedside table, she called out to him.

"Leave the light on."

He glanced over his shoulder at her, a frown on his face. "You won't be able to get back to sleep if I do."

"Yes, I will." She had no intention of sleeping again, but telling him would only provoke an argument. "If you think it will keep you from sleeping, maybe you should go to your room."

He straightened. "I'm staying." He returned to the couch and settled himself on it with her in his arms.

At first she lay stiffly, determined not to allow herself to give way to sleep. Dreams lay in sleep. Darkness too. And she had had enough of both. But gradually the heat from his body soaked into her and she relaxed and slept.

* * *

The next morning Angelica awoke alone on the couch, and in an instant everything that had happened the night before came rushing back to her. Appalled and embarrassed, she shut her eyes and covered her face with her hand. She had screamed at Amarillo not to touch her, then rushed to the bathroom and practically scrubbed the skin from her face. There she had fought him again. Finally he had had to bodily carry her from the bathroom.

He must have thought she was completely demented. He'd be justified in thinking so, her actions had been those of a crazy person.

Slowly she rose from the couch and went to shower and dress. When she returned to the bedroom, she found Amarillo sitting in front of a breakfast-laden table.

He smiled at her. "Good morning. I hope you're hungry. I ordered everything I could think of."

She eyed him cautiously. He looked so fresh and vital and full of energy, as if he were up to any challenge. It was the exact opposite of what she felt. "I don't think I want anything to eat just yet."

He pointed toward a plate of croissants and fruit. "How about something light?"

She smiled faintly. "You're still trying to feed me."

"That must be because I still think you need to eat."

"Don't worry about me," she said airily. "Losing a few pounds wouldn't hurt me at all."

"It would hurt me."

"Why?"

"Because—" he stopped, unsure of what he wanted to say. He stared at her for a moment, then stood and came to her and framed her face with his hands. "You look pale."

"I'm fine."

The strain of her expression told him that she wasn't. He frowned. "Maybe you should see a doctor."

"Because of a little nightmare? Don't be silly." She broke away from him and walked to the table. "I don't see anything chocolate here."

"You're changing the subject."

"I never get far away from the subject of chocolate."

"That was more than a little nightmare, Angelica, and we both know it."

With a sigh she turned back around. "Okay. Yes, yes, it was, but I don't want to talk about it. And I don't want you worrying about it."

"Worrying about it? You scared the hell out of me last night, Angelica."

Of course she had, she thought with self-disgust. She had acted like a madwoman. "I'm so sorry. So *truly* sorry. I think tonight it would be better if you slept in your room. That way you won't be disturbed."

"To hell with my being disturbed! You're the one I'm concerned about."

She pressed fingers to her temple. "I really don't want to talk about this."

"Angelica—"

"No." She wheeled and headed for the door. "I'm

going to see if the chef can whip up something chocolate for me, and then I'm going to get to work. I have a lot to do today."

"Angelica."

His voice stopped her before she reached the door. She looked over her shoulder.

"I'll be here tonight."

"There's no need. I'll be quite safe. I'll even lock the door."

"I'll be here tonight."

Angelica threw herself with gusto into the final plans for the ball, following up on the tiniest detail and making work when there was none. Anything to keep her mind from switching to the contents of her dreams.

She felt as if she were being haunted. She didn't know what the dreams meant, but they were so vivid, so utterly clear, it was as if they weren't really dreams at all. And that was at night. During the day they had begun to consume her.

Every once in a while she would look up from whatever she happened to be doing at the moment and she would see Amarillo watching her. She accepted his vigilance. She would not allow guards, and so he was keeping track of her. As long as she didn't feel closed in, she wouldn't complain, and he was obviously smart enough to know it.

He sensed danger and it was his nature to be a protector.

She, too, sensed danger, but an internal danger

that was more frightening to her than whatever the man who had been calling had planned for her.

Intellectually she knew her dreams *must* be connected in some way to the calls and the note. She was being harassed by some unknown person, and it was logical that the distress she felt would manifest itself in her dreams.

Up to a point, everything made sense.

Except—inside her there was a certain knowledge she couldn't explain or justify, a knowledge that was telling her that the dreams had very little to do with the calls and the note.

That evening she chose to eat in the dining room. She wanted to be around people, to hear them as they talked and laughed. She wanted to pretend she was, like them, completely normal.

Amarillo joined her at her table, elegant, charming, and very determined to be with her. He was silent for the most part, and she concentrated on eating, resolved he would have no cause to try to make her eat. After dinner they drifted apart as they mingled with the guests.

She was staving off that time when she would have to go upstairs to sleep. Eventually, though, her eyelids began to grow heavy, and suddenly Amarillo was beside her, taking her arm and leading her to the elevator.

"I suppose you're going to insist on coming to my room tonight," she said, leaning against the burgundy velvet padded walls of the elevator interior and gazing at him.

He nodded. "That's right."

"You can sleep in the same bed with me if you want, but I'm not going to make love with you."

"Whatever you want is fine with me," he said, the expression in his golden eyes solemn. Then he stepped to her, lowered his body against hers so that she was pressed against the velvet padded wall, and kissed her.

"Now what do you want?" he whispered against her mouth a moment later.

"You," she answered. "Lord, I want you."

And several hours passed before she slept and dreamed.

There was the darkness again, the fear, the crying. There was the music, the laughter, and the voices. And everything was mixed together with a surrealistic horror—the laughter with the crying, the music with the fear, the voices with the darkness.

She awoke with a gasp, and for a minute lay perfectly still, trying to separate reality from the dream. She was awake, she assured herself, not still caught up in the dark, intricate labyrinth of her subconscious.

Beside her she heard the deep, steady breathing of Amarillo. She gave silent thanks for the further reassurance she wasn't dreaming and for the fact that she hadn't awakened him.

As quietly as possible, she slipped from the bed, and taking the lace coverlet with her, she made her way to the open French door. Wrapping the coverlet around her, she sat down on the floor and rested her back against the doorjamb.

From the bed Amarillo watched her from beneath half-closed eyes. She looked so fragile, so vulnerable, his heart ached. With every minute, with every hour, she was withdrawing more and more from him. And he didn't know how to stop her.

A huge silver moon hung out over the water, lighting the night. Angelica focused on it, concentrating hard on its beauty and its mystery. By doing that, she didn't have to think about a horrible truth: She was losing her mind.

Eight

Peter came up behind Angelica as she was sitting in a second-floor meeting area, going through her notes. "Miss DiFrenza?"

Angelica started and jerked around. "What *is* it?"

The young bellman's eyes widened at her reaction. "I'm sorry. Am I bothering you?"

Angelica sighed. She was tired and her nerves were strung to the breaking point, but that was no reason to take it out on him, she realized. "No, Peter, you aren't bothering me, and I'm sorry I snapped at you."

He grinned with relief. "Don't worry about it. I know with the ball tomorrow night you must have a lot on your mind."

"I do, but that's no excuse. At any rate, what can I do for you?"

"Oh, right!" He grinned again, thinking that a guy could be forgiven for losing his train of thought just by looking at her. She was great, not to mention gorgeous. He mentally brought himself up short. She was also a Deverell and that took her way out of his league. "I came up to tell you that Mr. Breckinridge has checked in and wanted you to be told he'd arrived."

She nodded. "Thank you. I do want to speak with him. Could you call his room for me and ask him if now would be a good time for him to meet me? Here?"

"Sure will, Miss DiFrenza. Anything else I can do to help?

She graced him with a smile. "I'd love a pot of tea. And if you wouldn't mind, have the kitchen add several cups to the tray. I'm setting up shop here for a while. The guests for the ball have started arriving, and I don't have time right now to greet everyone. Oh, and see if the kitchen has any chocolate bars."

"No problem, Miss DiFrenza. Tea and chocolate bars it is."

Minutes later, when William Breckinridge appeared, Angelica did her best to shake off her strained mood, even though she noted that he appeared to be under somewhat of a strain himself. "I hope your trip was pleasant and uneventful."

"Yes, it was, thank you. The jewels are locked away in a safe I had brought in and placed in the room I've been assigned, and I've already sent back to Boston the guard who accompanied me here."

A sudden thought occurred to her. "Did I remember to tell you that Mr. Smith is handling the extra security here?"

"He notified me, and I plan to check in with him just as soon as you and I are through."

As usual his formality was getting her down, and she decided to try to interject some lightness into their conversation. "It sounds as if you have everything under control. I hope you plan to utilize some of SwanSea's facilities while you're here. Do you play tennis?"

"No, I'm afraid I don't, but I'm sure I'll find plenty to keep myself busy."

She tried to imagine him walking along the beach, picking up seashells, and failed completely. "That's good. By the way, sometime today I would like to get the rubies."

Dismay puckered his brow. "I'm not sure that would be wise, Miss DiFrenza. They should stay in the safe right up until the time you plan to wear them. That's the procedure I follow with all the ladies."

"I see. Well, I'll speak with Mr. Smith about it. At any rate, I'm glad you and the jewels have arrived safely. And now that you're here, try to relax and have a good time."

A strange expression crossed his face, and he seemed to hesitate. He was probably trying to decide if he should tell her that his idea of a good time would be to sit in front of the vault all day and watch it, she thought, then immediately chastised herself. He was a valued employee of DiFrenza's and had been for years. She just wished he weren't so tiring.

"Good-bye, Mr. Breckinridge."

"Good-bye, Miss DiFrenza."

*   *   *

By late afternoon Angelica had a pounding headache, a still uncompleted list of things she needed to do, and a growing sense that the walls were closing in around her. Barely conscious of making the decision to flee, she escaped the house by a back door and headed toward the woods.

The day was warm, the breeze gentle. Quite a few people were out, strolling through the gardens, heading to and from the swimming pool and the tennis courts, or simply sitting on the lawn in padded lounge chairs, enjoying the view and the sun. The latter activity appealed greatly to her, and she wondered fleetingly if it was possible for the sun to bake away the demons that seemed to be filling her head and giving her the dreams.

Sometime later, Amarillo found her stretched out on a soft, luxuriant section of grass by a clear running brook, an arm across her closed eyes. He quietly lowered himself to the ground beside her.

She felt his presence as an increase in warmth on her skin and an acceleration of her pulse, but she had mixed emotions about his being there. She didn't feel fit to be around anyone, especially him. For him she wanted to be at her best, and she was anything but that now.

During the past half hour she had been going over and over her dreams, trying to find a thread of reason within their chaos.

Who was the child who cried? Who was the man who handled her so roughly? And who was the lady with the sweet, familiar voice? She should *know*, but she had racked her brain and had come up with no memories. In the end, she had succeeded only in increasing her anxiety and tension.

"How did you find me?" she asked without moving her arm.

"Peter saw you go into the woods. I think he has a crush on you."

"He's a nice boy."

"I'm sure he wouldn't be thrilled to hear you call him a boy."

Slowly she lowered her arms and opened her eyes. "Was there some reason in particular you wanted to see me?" She couldn't believe what she was saying even as she was saying it. Her aloof tone was even harder to believe. It reinforced what she already knew—she had found no peace here by the brook, and the state of her nerves was at a critical point. Dear Lord, *was there any hope for her?*

His gaze narrowed on her. "There are a lot of reasons, the main one being I don't like you out of my sight too long."

"You really do need to curb those protective tendencies of yours, Amarillo."

"I can't seem to do that, at least not with you," he said, unperturbed by her sarcasm. "How are things going?"

She sat up, wishing she could open up and tell him everything she was thinking—that she wasn't doing at all well, that bit by bit she was losing control, and that soon she would be completely insane. But she loved him too much to burden him with her problems. . . .

"I really can't complain, although today's been a little hectic," she said lightly. "I got a call from Boston, telling me that one of my buyers, who's in Italy buying for the fall season, has fallen in love with an Italian." She shrugged. "Go figure. He pinched her bottom and won her heart. She quit on the spot. Seems she's going to redirect her life. The message was a little garbled, but it had to do with sports cars, pasta, and bambinos. I had to dispatch someone to replace her. Then the florist called to tell me that his number one assistant has developed an allergy to flowers and won't be able to help him tomorrow. He's frantic and assures me he can't go on." She checked her watch. "An hour and a half ago the confection chef got in a huff because his grocery order was short four bags of sugar and he stormed out of the kitchen, vowing never to return. But all in all, it's going really well."

"That's good."

She met his gaze, half expecting to see the familiar twinkle of humor in his eye. Instead, she saw concern. "Hey, I'll handle it somehow, and I have every faith that tomorrow night there will be a ball."

"I couldn't care less about the damned ball, Angelica."

It was the dreams, she thought with sudden dread. He was going to ask her about the dreams, and she wouldn't be able to stand it. She felt physically and mentally incapable of voicing her fears and confusion at this point. She had just been through it with herself, and the ordeal had left her feeling scraped raw. Besides, he deserved better than to be dragged into the horrible twists and turns of her mind, especially when she herself didn't know what was there.

She rushed to another subject. "Have you come up with anything on the man who has been harassing me?"

"Not a thing. I have our people in Boston working on it. The police are running his method of operation through the computer, the note has been sent to the lab, and the tap is still on your phone. But so far nothing."

"It's been three days since he sent the note. Maybe he's given up."

"I'd like to believe that, but I don't. Not for a minute. I think he knows I'm involved and is trying to figure out the best way to get around me."

A chill ran down her spine. "That sounds very ruthless."

"You better believe it." He paused. "Have you given any more thought to who this man could be?"

She drew her legs up and wrapped her arms around them. "No."

Suddenly he let out a string of curses. "I can't take any more of this. Talk to me, Angelica."

She looked at him in surprise. "I thought I was."

"No. You're talking, but not to me. Ever since the dreams have gotten worse, you've pulled away from me and withdrawn into yourself. I'm sure what's happening with you isn't obvious to other people, but it's damned obvious to me. And if I let things go on as they have been, pretty soon I won't be able to reach you at all."

"I don't know what you're talking about."

"Yes, you do." He put a finger beneath her chin and turned her face so that she had to look at him. "Tell me what's in these damn dreams of yours and why they bother you so much."

She shook her head, dislodging his finger. "I can't. Don't ask me."

"I have to ask you. Something is hurting you badly, but I can't help you if you don't let me know what it is."

"Did you ever think that there are some things you simply can't fix, Amarillo?"

"No. Never."

Her laugh held pain. "It must be nice." She put her hands on the ground to push herself up, but he grabbed her.

"Don't run away from me."

She stayed where she was, because the hand on her arm wouldn't let her do anything else. And because she detected a hint of aching in his voice. "Amarillo, this doesn't concern you."

His golden eyes glittered fiercely. "You're wrong. There's no reason why you should be struggling through whatever this is alone. Somehow I have to find a way to convince you of that, somehow I have to find a way to reach into you and help you."

How could she make him understand what was happening inside her mind when she couldn't understand it herself? How could she say to him, *I'm going mad*? She couldn't and survive the trauma. Saying it aloud would make it a reality.

Not only couldn't she bring herself to face it, she wouldn't be able to bear it if he knew something so horrible about her.

She wanted to throw herself into his arms and give up all her burdens to him, but she refused to let herself. He was the kind of man who solved difficult problems with the same ease as other men swatted flies. But there was no way he could solve her problem. Demons were inside her, playing games with her mind—and only she could fight them.

Most men would be happy to have a smile from her, Amarillo thought, watching her. To be her lover would be more than most of them would ever expect in life. But he was finding, much to his astonishment, that he wouldn't be satisfied with less than all of her.

Her continued silence was the final shove that pushed him over the edge, and his grip tightened on her arms. "Dammit, Angelica, for the past two days you've put more and more distance between us, and I won't let it continue. I *can't*."

She would give everything she owned to be able to explain to him what was happening, to help him understand, to put him out of his misery. But she had to be able to help herself before she could help anyone else, and right now she didn't know if that was possible. "I'm sorry, Amarillo. I wish I could help you."

He jerked her to him. "You wish you could help me? *Help* me?"

"I'm sorry."

"Stop saying that! Give me an enemy to fight, Angelica. I'm a hell of a fighter. And I always win.

Dammit, *I love you!*" For a moment he stopped breathing. He didn't know where the word *love* had come from, he thought, badly jolted. But then his breathing resumed, and he knew he meant it with all his heart. "I love you," he said, this time with deep gentleness.

She was stunned. And then her heart began to tear in two. His love was something for which she had unconsciously yearned for years. If at any time in the past he had told her that he loved her, she would have been ecstatic. This past week she would have been over the moon. But not now, not since the dreams had started to come alive in her mind, not since they had started to drag her into this screaming, unceasing nightmare that had begun to last night and day.

"Usually when a man tells a woman he loves her, he gets some response."

"Really? Has that been your experience?" She had sounded cruel, but it hadn't been intentional. She just didn't know what to say.

"Angelica, I've told only one other woman that I loved her in my entire life, and that was my wife."

"I'm honored. I really am, but—"

He put a finger over her mouth. "Don't say it."

"What?"

"Don't say you don't love me. I don't want to hear it. Not now, at any rate."

She had no intention of telling him she didn't love him. It would be impossible for her to get the words past her throat. "I'm sorry," she whispered.

"No," he said harshly, gently caressing her

cheek. "There's nothing for you to be sorry about, because you *are* going to love me."

His assurance was wonderful, she thought lovingly. *He* was wonderful. Dammit, why did she have to be so screwed up?

"For years I stayed away from you because I wanted to keep you safe. Then I let myself get too close to you and immediately catapulted head over heels in love. The irony there is that I had already been in love with you for years. But then, to complicate matters, I found out someone is threatening you, and it has nothing whatsoever to do with me or my job, the very thing that made me stay away from you in the first place. Another irony, a real irony, don't you think?"

"Yes."

He reached out and framed her face with his hands. "I can do something about this jerk who's bothering you, Angelica. I *am* doing something. But now I have a new, added problem—there's an internal threat in addition to the external threat to you. And I don't find it ironic at all. Something's going on inside you, Angelica, that's apparently even scarier to you than this guy."

"You understand that?" she asked, amazed.

"Yes, honey, I do, but I can't do anything about it, because you won't tell me about it." His face was drawn tight with frustration and anger. "I don't know what to do anymore, and I'm really lousy at doing nothing."

He couldn't help her, she thought. No one could. But his understanding and love meant more than she could say. Just like the child in her dream, she had been feeling so all alone. Now perhaps the biggest irony of all was that she wasn't in a position to accept either his love or his understanding. Tears came to her eyes. "It's funny, I hardly ever cry, but lately tears seem to come so easily."

"Everyone should cry once in a while. It's good for them."

"So is laughing. Make me laugh."

"Let's go strip-wading in the brook."

Surprise made her burst out laughing. *"What?"*

"Let's take off all our clothes and go wading in the brook."

She chuckled. "For some reason I expected a joke, not a proposition, but I think it's a great idea, and you made me laugh. Thank you. Now what can I do for you?"

His patience was in tatters, yet he knew that pushing her in any way would be a mistake. But he needed her, oh, how he needed her. "Make love to me."

She gazed into his eyes and saw that they were totally devoid of laughter. "Now?"

"Here and now," he said huskily. "I want you."

She curved her arms around his neck and fell forward against him so that her body weight pushed him backward. He put his arms around her and took her down to the sweet-smelling grass.

She had undermined everything he had ever thought important in himself, every self-protective instinct he'd ever possessed, every bit of control he had ever thought necessary.

Now only she was important and necessary to him.

He felt her exploring his body with her hands and her lips, and he had to grit his teeth at the feelings that were sweeping through him.

"I've changed my mind," he said, stilling her. Then he rolled over until he was on top of her. "I want to make love to you, so thoroughly and for so long you'll be too weak to fight me anymore. Then I'll make love to you some more until you can't do anything but trust me and tell me what in the hell is the matter."

She felt sad because she couldn't tell him what he wanted to hear, and at the same time she wanted him desperately. "Let's make love to each other," she murmured.

"That's a hell of an idea."

He wanted to be gentle with her, but his anger and frustration churned and mixed with his growing passion, making it impossible to take his time.

They tore at each other's clothes until they were naked, panting, and clinging to each other. And when he joined their bodies, Angelica felt a storm of fire and passion rush through her, and she arched up to him. In this, at least, she could give completely. And she did, holding nothing back.

Angelica smiled as she emerged from the shower and reached for a towel. She even found herself humming a little tune. The smile and the tune were both, she knew, a direct consequence of the afternoon she had spent with Amarillo by the brook.

After their lovemaking, they had gone wading

in the brook. They had laughed and splashed each other with water like children. Later they had made love again, and she felt an extraordinary satisfaction with the knowledge that they had really made *love*.

He had told her he loved her. She was still amazed. There had been a time not too long ago when she had thought it impossible to hear such an admission from him.

She viewed his love as a miracle.

She would need another miracle to be able to accept it.

But just having him tell her of his love had made her feel stronger and had given her new hope.

As she looked back over the last few days, she was vaguely puzzled. It wasn't like her to be a defeatist, to simply cave in when faced with adversity. But, no matter, she didn't blame herself. It showed her how powerful the dreams were. They came from a deep, dark, terrifying place inside her, and they were finding and striking at wounds she had not realized she had.

She dried herself off and donned the short violet robe. Amarillo had gone to his room to make a few phone calls, but he soon would join her, and her heart was racing with the anticipation of seeing him again. Somehow—for his sake, for hers, for *theirs*—she had to fight and overcome what was happening to her. She would go to a psychiatrist for help. The knowledge of Amarillo's love should be making this the happiest time of her life. She wasn't going to be cheated of this time, and she *wasn't* going to fall apart.

She didn't doubt that there would be another dream tonight. But this time she would handle it better. And the one tomorrow night. And the one the next night. Until soon she would be able to understand and handle what was happening to her, and then she would be able to tell him she loved him.

She belted the robe at the waist, strolled into the bedroom, and headed for the wardrobe and an outfit that would see her through the rest of the afternoon until dinner. It might be fun, she thought, opening the closet door, to have dinner down in the dining room again.

She reached for a pair of slacks and a blouse, then saw her red-violet ballgown hanging to one side. The lovely silk-taffeta material had been slashed time after time from neckline to hem.

She screamed.

Amarillo, who was just coming into the room, reached her in four long strides. "What—" He saw the gown and let out a string of fluent curses. The ballgown was in shreds. He reached for her. "Are you all right?" At her nod he asked, "Did you see who did this?"

"No," she said, and gave a short prayer of thanks she hadn't. Whoever had done this was obviously a dangerous person.

"When was the last time you looked into this wardrobe?"

She drew a deep breath, trying to compose herself. But the sight of something so beautiful that had been deliberately ruined had her shaking. "This morning when I was dressing."

"And then you left for the day and didn't return

until just a few minutes ago when we came upstairs together?"

"That's right."

"Did you lock the door?"

She hesitated. "No."

"Dammit, Angelica. What did I tell you about locking your door?"

She gave a small cry. "Oh, for heaven's sake, what does it matter what you told me? My ball-gown is shredded. The real question is why would anyone do such a thing?"

"Why has he done anything he's done?" Amarillo asked grimly.

"*He?*" Her eyes widened. "You mean you think this was done by the same man who's been calling me?"

"Who else?"

"But that would mean—"

"That's right." His expression turned stone hard. "He's here."

Angelica couldn't escape the darkness or the terror. She heard herself crying. She was cold and dirty and small, very small. She heard the loud voices again.

"I thought you loved me," the man yelled.

"I do! You know I do."

It was the woman with the familiar voice. Angelica wanted to get to her. She beat her tiny fists against the door.

"Be a good girl," she heard the woman call through the door to her. Then she asked the man, "Why don't you let her out, let me see her, hold her, for just a little while? What would it hurt? Her little gown is ruined. I could clean her up."

"Just go back home, do what you're supposed to do, and quit worrying about the brat. Do as I say. I'm your golden-haired boy, aren't I?"

"Yes, oh, yes, you are."

"And you'll mind me, won't you?"

"Yes."

Then suddenly she was outside, sitting on the wet grass, and bushes were all around. It was nighttime, and she had never known such terror. And there was the color red. . . .

Angelica sat up in bed with a cry and stared around her. There was light—she remembered leaving on the bedside lamp—but the color of red shrouded everything, including her, like a haze. Was she awake? It was so hard to tell anymore.

Amarillo sat up, beside her but not touching her. His heart was pounding like a hammer. Her dreams couldn't frighten her any more than they frightened him, but he couldn't let her know. She had enough to deal with at the moment. "Angelica," he said softly, "it's all right. I'm right here with you."

She blinked, but the red wouldn't go away. It was a *violent* color, she thought with fear. A color of death. "I'm still dreaming."

"No, you're awake. Turn around and look at me."

"No." She was afraid to, afraid that if she did, he would resemble the faceless people in her dream. Afraid he would be colored over with red, afraid that if he was, she would never be able to stop screaming.

Determinedly she blinked again. The haze began to fade.

Where had the red come from, she wondered frantically. It had never been in her dreams before, nor had being outside on the damp grass. And then there was the fact that once again, even after she had awakened, the dream had still held her in its grip.

She was getting worse, she thought with sudden dread.

"I'm going to put my arms around you," she heard Amarillo say, and then felt him doing it.

He eased her against him and slid back against the headboard. "I know you want me to leave you alone," he whispered, his mouth against her temple, "but I can't do that, at least not now. I'm going to be here with you, and I'm going to stay until you're all right again. Until you're safe." He smoothed his hand over her arm. "Then if you want me to go away, I will."

Long after she had finally fallen asleep again, he continued holding her. It seemed to him as if his love should be able to solve anything for Angelica. There was so *much* of it; it was so strong. But no matter how hard he tried, he couldn't seem to help her.

It wasn't in him to give up, but he didn't know what to do next. And he had two new problems.

She hadn't told him she loved him. It would be impossible for her to love him as much as he loved her. The thing was, she didn't love him at all, and knowing that was probably the hardest thing with which he had ever had to deal. But he could handle it, he determined, as long as she stayed with him. Which brought him to his second problem.

He had said he would go away if she wanted him to. But if that time ever came, he didn't know how in hell he would be able to make himself do it.

He could live without her love, but he couldn't live without her.

Nine

With the single-minded determination of worker bees, people moved around the ballroom, carrying out their individual tasks. Armloads of flowers were being carried in and arranged by the florist and his assistants, including the newly hired one. The chairs, music stands, and instruments of the orchestra were being set up on the specially built stage. In one corner, a steel-nerved bartender arranged glasses in a pyramid for a champagne fountain.

Angelica viewed the commotion from the side of the room, where she sat at a table with Amarillo.

His eyes were narrowed as he surveyed the ballroom's occupants, subjecting each one to a laser-like inspection.

Watching him, her lips twisted with amusement. "You're making everyone extremely nervous, you know."

He looked over at her. "Why's that?"

"That stare of yours. It's like an X ray."

He shrugged. "It shouldn't bother anyone unless he or she is guilty of something."

"It's obvious you've never seen that particular expression of yours. It resembles something out of a Clint Eastwood movie—like, 'do one thing wrong and I'll drop you right where you stand.' "

He grinned. "You're exaggerating."

"Not even a little."

He reached out and caressed her cheek, a gesture, he realized, that had become a habit with him. "I'm glad to see you in such good spirits today."

She nodded, agreeing with him, but at the same time reflecting with sad resignation that her dream of last night was still very much with her, as was the moment when she had opened the closet door and seen her red-violet dress hanging in shreds. But she would fall apart if she allowed herself to dwell on it, and she couldn't let that happen. A life with Amarillo was worth fighting for, and that was just what she was going to do. "I think my good spirits come from sheer relief that the ball is tonight. I couldn't have taken one more day of things going wrong. Next year Caitlin gets this chore back. She has the organization of charity events down pat."

His hand fell from her cheek to grasp her hand. "You've done a great job."

She gave a pretend shudder. "Don't say that. Not yet. You'll jinx me."

"Not a chance. Everything's going to be great. You'll see."

"I hope you're right."

"I am, and I have some news that will be the icing on the cake. Metta is sending one of her sculptures down today by truck. She wants to donate it to be auctioned off tonight."

Excited, she clapped her hands together. "Why, that's great news! Everyone will break their neck bidding."

"That's the idea. *And* there's more. Beau has been persuaded to donate a catered dinner for twenty-four."

"Persuaded?"

He shrugged. "It was fairly easy."

The twinkle was back in his gold eyes, and she felt her heart turn over. "Have I told you lately that I think you're wonderful?"

"No, I don't think you have."

"You're wonderful. And as a reward, you don't have to stay with me."

He shook his head. "Sounds like a punishment to me."

She laughed. "What I mean is, I'm surrounded by people. Nothing's going to happen to me here."

"Maybe I like being with you."

"Uh-huh. Then why aren't you looking at me instead of giving the workers the third degree?"

"I don't have to look at you to be aware of you. I only have to breathe."

Everything about her softened, including her voice. "My, my, Mr. Smith. You do know exactly which buttons to push, don't you?"

He leaned toward her, his eyes glittering. "I don't know as many as I'd like to. Maybe we could go up to your room and I could learn some more."

"Oh, here you are, Miss DiFrenza. I've been looking for you."

Angelica's head jerked up at the sound of William Breckinridge's voice. He was immaculate and stylish in linen slacks, silk shirt, and a designer tie. "Is there something wrong?" she asked.

"No, no, but I heard something had happened to you, and I thought I should come make sure you were all right."

Her mind went momentarily blank. "What did you hear happened to me?"

"Not to you exactly, but to the ballgown that you had specially designed to go with the rubies—I heard it was slashed. It's quite shocking, a real tragedy."

As usual, he had managed to rub her the wrong way. "World hunger is a tragedy, Mr. Breckinridge, a ruined dress is a minor inconvenience."

To her surprise, he fidgeted uncomfortably. "Yes, of course, I just meant that now you won't be able to wear the rubies."

"Oh, I still plan to wear them. Yesterday I contacted the store and they've sent me another gown. As a matter of fact, they've sent me two identical gowns, just in case something happens to one."

He looked startled. "You mean they found two red-violet gowns to match the jewels?"

"No, unfortunately that would have been virtually impossible. The gowns they've sent me are black. The effect won't be quite as dramatic, but it will work well enough." She thought for a moment. "Actually, in some ways black may be even better. The red-violet of the rubies will stand out against the black more than it would have against the other gown."

He clasped his hands tightly together. "Well, I'm glad everything has worked out for you. Uh, is there anything I can do to help you here?"

"No, everything is under control. You should go enjoy yourself. Have you looked around the grounds, checked out the facilities?"

"No, no."

Her teeth came together in exasperation. "Mr. Breckinridge, you did come in a day early. You should take advantage of the extra time you have and relax."

The grip he held on his hands tightened. "Coming in a day early was probably a miscalculation on my part. I thought I would have more duties, but as it turns out I was wrong. However, I'll be glad to pay my night's room rate instead of charging it to DiFrenza's."

She sighed. "For heaven's sake, don't worry about the room rate. Have fun." She checked her watch. It was just after ten in the morning. "Our guests will probably start dressing around six. You have until late afternoon." She paused. "However, I may check with you sooner. I meant to before now, but I've been so busy I forgot about it. Anyway, I'm really dying to see the rubies again." She threw Amarillo a quick smile. "And I can't wait for Amarillo to see them. But, listen, don't stay in on our account. We'll come find you when we're ready."

"Well, then, if you're sure there's nothing I can help with, I'll be going."

She waited until he was out of earshot, then turned to Amarillo. "We won't have to look too hard for him. He'll be in his room."

"What do you mean?" he asked, his gaze following William Breckinridge as he left the ballroom.

She shook her head. "Forget I said anything. That was catty of me. It's just that of all the DiFrenza employees, he's the one I like least. He's such a stuffed shirt."

"Tell me something. Has he ever served as escort for the jewelry before? I mean here to SwanSea."

"Sure. He's done it for the last few years—since Caitlin opened SwanSea as a resort and she and Nico reunited the Deverells and the DiFrenzas."

"That's interesting."

"Believe me, there's nothing interesting about him."

"I disagree. I think it's extremely interesting that he said he misjudged and came in a day early. If he's done this before, he should know how much of his time is required for the job."

She looked at him. "You know what? You've been a detective too long."

"But I'm wonderful. You just said so."

"I did, didn't I? I must have forgotten." She sent him a quick grin. "Oh, there's Peter. *Peter!*"

The young man hurried over. "Miss DiFrenza, Mr. Smith."

She smiled at him and wondered if he knew that Alice, a young woman who worked at the front desk, practically melted every time he looked her way. "Hi, Peter. I just wanted to let you know that I'll probably be here most of the morning, so if you'd bring any messages here, I'd appreciate it."

He grinned. "No problem, Miss DiFrenza. And what about some tea and chocolate bars?"

Amarillo held up an admonishing hand. "You can bring her the messages, but all mail and packages go through me, right?"

Peter's grin vanished, and his spine straightened, giving the impression he was a young military officer coming to attention before the general. "Yes, sir, Mr. Smith. Just like you said."

"Peter," Angelica said gently. "Tea and chocolate bars would really be great. Thank you for thinking of it." When the young man had gone, she turned to Amarillo. "Shame on you. You intimidated poor Peter."

"He can bring you all the tea and chocolate bars he wants. But I wanted to make sure he understood about everything else. This guy who's been bothering you sent you a clear message yesterday when he slashed your ballgown. He doesn't want you to go to the ball. Now, if I'm right about that, then you'll hear from him sometime today."

The thought sent chills coursing down her spine. Determinedly she put on a bright face. "On the other hand, we could take an optimistic view and say that he's given up and gone away."

In the face of her resolute bravery, his expression gentled. "You take the optimistic view, I'll do the worrying. That's my job."

"Oh, your *job*," she said with a teasing lilt to her voice. "Am I paying you?"

In a surprise move he leaned over and kissed her. "One smile pays any and all debts to me."

A sweet warmth flooded her. "Weren't we just talking about buttons?"

"Yes, we were," he murmured close to her ear. "That and seeing what we could do about finding more. Upstairs, in your room."

She groaned. "I'd love to, but the ball—"

He pulled away. "I'll be so glad when this damned ball is over."

She gave a rueful chuckle. "No more than I will be. But listen, there's no reason why we should both suffer. You don't need to stay here with me. Like I said, I'm surrounded by people, and you've already subjected them to your X-ray vision."

He grinned. "I'll stay awhile, but later I may go for a ride." Without telling Angelica, the day before he had sent for five of his best men. Two of them were in the ballroom now. Three others were stationed in various spots in and around SwanSea. "My horses are getting jealous. Normally when I'm here, they have my whole attention." He shook his head solemnly. "They're sensing there's someone else."

She burst out with a loud laugh. "That's just great! For years I had to watch you with one glamorous woman after another, and now I'm in competition with *horses*."

He leaned toward her again. "Honey, you have *no* competition."

Later that afternoon Angelica decided that everything was as ready as she could make it. If something wasn't done by now, it simply didn't matter. She felt a flush of accomplishment, because despite the dreams, despite the harassment, she had managed to carry on and oversee what had every indication of being a successful charity event. She felt good about the upcoming ball and herself.

In a fairly upbeat mood, she went to find Amarillo. When she was told he was riding, she strolled out onto a side veranda. In the distance she saw him astride a golden palomino.

She perched on the balustrade and watched him. They were beautiful, she thought, the man and his horse, both golden, both strong and moving in perfect rhythm along the bluff that overlooked the ocean. Her heart swelled. He made her so happy, and she loved him more than she had ever thought it possible to love anyone. They *had* to have a chance for happiness. She had to beat the specter of the dreams. She just wished she knew how.

"Miss DiFrenza?"

She glanced around to see Peter, bearing several messages and a package.

"Hi, Peter." She automatically took the messages from him and glanced through them. She was relieved to see that most of the messages were invitations for drinks before the dinner tonight instead of people calling about problems. She finished shuffling through the messages and pointed to the taped box he held. "What's that?"

"It's for you, but Mr. Smith told me all packages are to go to him first."

"That's right. Well, as you can see for yourself, he's riding." She pointed toward the bluff. "Why don't you leave the package with me and I'll give it to him when he comes in. You can set it down here." She patted the balustrade in front of her.

"I guess that would be all right."

"Sure." She smiled at him. "And, Peter, thanks for being so much help to me these last few days."

He broke into a wide, beaming grin. 'It was *my* pleasure, Miss DiFrenza."

"You know, there's a young woman at the front desk, I think her name is Alice. Do you know her?"

"I know her, but not real well. Why?"

"Oh, no reason. I just think she's really pretty, that's all."

"You do?"

"Uh-huh. Thanks again, Peter."

"Oh, no problem."

She turned around and saw that Amarillo was looking in her direction. She waved. He waved back and reined his horse toward the house.

Smiling happily, watching him come toward her, she idly reached for the box and plucked at the tape with her fingernail until she could grip it and peel it off. She was folding back the flaps just as Amarillo dismounted at the base of the terrace.

He vaulted over the balustrade. *"What are you doing?"*

"N-nothing," she said, surprised at his furious expression.

"God, it's ticking!" He grabbed the box away from her, but not before she had glanced into it and seen its contents.

"It's a clock, Amarillo." She tried to grab it back, but he held the box tight, staring hard at the clock, and she leaned forward so she could see too. It was a small crystal and mother-of-pearl clock, the type a woman would keep on her dresser. "Why, it's lovely! I wonder who would have sent me a clock."

"There wasn't a card?"

"No. Here, let me have it."

She reached out for the box, but Amarillo didn't release it, and he couldn't tear his gaze from the clock. He felt as if he were encased in ice, completely immobilized, but his mind was working at the speed of light.

The clock was lovely; its mother-of-pearl face and gold hands gleamed in the afternoon sunlight. The second hand ticked off the seconds. One . . . two . . . three . . .

Amarillo straightened and threw the box as far out over the grounds as he could, then he grabbed Angelica and pulled her to the floor of the veranda behind the balustrade.

The shock and fall took her breath away. "What—?"

He wrapped his arms around her and held her tight against him.

The explosion was loud and the percussion stunning. Tiny bits of the clock landed on the veranda with a clatter, along with clumps of grass.

The explosion. Angelica put her hands over her ears. She heard another explosion in her head. Where was it coming from? Was it another bomb? No, it was part of the dream.

No! It *couldn't* be.

She was awake, she was definitely awake. She

refused to let herself go off the deep end now, not when she had so much to remain sane for. She heard Amarillo speak to her.

"Are you all right?"

His tone was low and throbbing. "I guess so." She laughed shakily. "How did you know?"

He stood and drew her to her feet. "Instinct more than anything else." He glanced toward the black hole the bomb had made in the green grass, then back to her. "My guess is it was plastique with a photosensitive device set to go off after ten to twelve seconds of exposure to light. I'll know more after I study it."

"Thank heaven for your instincts. I don't even know why I opened the package. I didn't intend to. I was going to wait until you got through riding and give it to you. And then I was watching you and . . ."

His eyes darkened with anger as he gazed at her and realized she had nearly been killed. Her face was deathly white, and it was clear only her will was keeping her from crumbling. He pulled her into his arms and hugged her tight. "If anything had happened to you—" The rest of the words knotted in his throat.

He wanted to keep on holding her, shielding her with his body, protecting her from anything that might hurt her. But out of the corner of his eye he noticed people had begun to come out of the house. They were talking excitedly and pointing toward the explosion site. He loosened his hold on Angelica and turned to the people. "There's nothing to worry about, folks. I was playing with some fireworks, thinking we might have a few tonight, but one got away from me, that's all. Nothing to worry about. Now that I've had time to consider, I don't think fireworks for tonight is a real good idea."

The people in the crowd laughed and repeated what he had said to others who were coming out on the veranda. They milled around, then slowly began dispersing.

Amarillo spotted three of his men converging on them and gave them a sign that had them disappearing into the shadows. Then he saw Peter and motioned him over. He put his hand on the young man's shoulder. "I have a very important job that I need you to do for me, and the job calls for the utmost discretion. Can I depend on you for this?"

"Yes, *sir!*"

"Good. Now, listen very carefully. The box you gave Miss DiFrenza exploded—"

"Oh, no!"

Amarillo's hand tightened on his shoulder. "It's all right. She wasn't hurt. But I want you to get one other person, a friend of yours you can trust, and comb this area"—a sweep of his hand included the veranda and the grounds in front of it—"for pieces of the clock and any other thing that looks odd or out of place. Can you do that?"

Peter nodded solemnly. "Yes, sir. I won't let you down."

"I knew I could depend on you." He turned to Angelica, slid his arm around her, and began walking with her back into the house. "How does a hot bath sound?"

She tilted her head to his shoulder. "With or without you?"

"Without this time. I want to come back down here, but first I want to make sure you're all right."

"Oh, I'm fine."

"Don't lie to me, Angelica," he said gently. "I know your legs must be about to give way on you."

Her laugh was shaky. "How did you get so smart?"

"I fell in love with you."

Outwardly she smiled; inwardly she agonized. *Why did she keep hearing the explosion over and over in her mind?* She would like to think that under the circumstances it was a normal thing to happen. But she was very much afraid it was another sign of her diminishing sanity.

Amarillo closed and locked Angelica's door and nodded to the man standing just outside it. "I shouldn't be gone long. But until I get back, no one is to be let in unless I okay it. And if for some reason that I can't think of Angelica leaves the room, follow her, but try not to be obvious."

The man grimaced. "Blending into the woodwork is going to be pretty hard to do, seeing as how I'm the only other person on this floor at the moment."

He lightly slapped the man's arm. "You're one of the best. That's why I sent for you."

Too impatient to wait for the private elevator, Amarillo headed for the back stairway.

As he made short work of the four flights of stairs, he reflected that he had tried hard to respect Angelica's wishes and not assign body-guards to her, but in the end, protecting her life had come first. This was the first time he had asked one of the men specifically to watch her. But even if she never spoke to him again because of it, he had had no choice. As much as he had loved his wife, he had survived her death. He wouldn't be able to survive Angelica's.

He exited a side door of the house, his intent to find out if one of his men who had been out-side at the time of the explosion might have seen someone watching Angelica as she had sat on the veranda. He was sure that whoever had sent her the clock would have wanted to see the results.

Out of the corner of his eye he sensed move-ment. He turned and saw William Breckinridge walking fast toward the parking area. Frowning, Amarillo glanced at his watch. It was very near the time when the women would be wanting the jewelry they had chosen to wear for the evening. His eyes narrowed, and he set out after the man.

"Breckinridge! Hold up!"

The jeweler whirled around, startled and wary. Studying him, Amarillo thought Breckinridge's expression resembled that of a wild animal who had just realized he's in danger. But Breckinridge wasn't looking down the barrel of a high-powered rifle as a wild animal might. So why was he so wary?

"Where are you going?" Amarillo asked, walking up to him.

An intended nonchalant gesture was hampered by the fact that he carried a suitcase. "Nowhere. Just to my car."

"You wouldn't by any chance be leaving, would you?"

"No, no. I was just going to put my suitcase in my car so that I would be ready to leave first thing in the morning."

"That's very efficient. I wonder why I'm bothered? Maybe because I don't think a three-day visit requires that much organization, suitcase-wise. Maybe because I have a strange feeling you're leaving now."

"Now? Oh, no." He shook his head vehemently. "No, no."

"Good. Then I'll stay here while you put your suitcase in the car, and then we'll go back to your room together. I'd like to have a look at the jewelry."

"I assure you that's not necessary. The jewelry is completely safe."

Amarillo smiled thinly. "Then it will all be there, won't it?"

Angelica walked across the room to the ringing phone, the silk of her black ballgown rustling, a cloud of perfume following her. For a moment her hand hovered over the phone, then she chided herself. She hadn't received one of those weird phone calls in days. She had just had a bomb delivered to her, that was all. "Hello?"

"Hi," Amarillo said. "What took you so long? Were you still in the bath?"

"No. I decided I wasn't in the mood for a long soak. In fact, I'm already dressed."

"Good, because I'd like you to come down to William Breckinridge's room."

"Why? Is there something wrong?" Her hand flew to her heart. "Oh, my Lord, the jewelry hasn't been stolen, has it?"

"No, it's all here. Just come down, will you? Oh, and—now, Angelica, don't get upset—but you're going to find a man outside your door. He works for Nico and me. Have him escort you."

She glanced at the door and felt something cold slide down her spine. *Someone was out there, and he was gong to hurt her.*

She closed her eyes. What was wrong with her? Assigning a man to guard her was a perfectly natural thing for Amarillo to do, and the man wouldn't hurt her.

"Angelica?"

"All right. I need to get the jewelry I'm going to wear tonight anyway. I'll be there in a few minutes."

The walk down the hall to the private elevator, and then the elevator ride from the fourth floor to the third, seemed to take forever. Her nerves were strung tighter than they'd ever been before, her stomach was in knots. Someone had actually tried to *kill* her. She had never had an enemy in her life that she knew of.

She was still hearing the explosion in her mind, and every time she did, it terrified her. And somehow she felt her fear went beyond what had happened that afternoon. In the folds of her black silk gown her hands balled into fists.

Don't let it get to you, she cautioned herself. *You have to quit thinking about it. Just get through the evening ahead.*

At William Breckinridge's room she found another guard. He nodded at her, knocked on the door, then opened it for her. When she walked in, she saw a grim-faced Amarillo standing across the room from an ashen William Breckinridge.

Amarillo motioned his two men inside and pointed toward the stack of jewelry cases on the bed. "Take the cases down by the elevator. There are chairs and a table there." He paused to draw a list out of his pocket. "This is a list of names of who will be coming for the jewelry, plus what sets they are to have. Be sure to check them off."

The men nodded, took the cases and the list, and left. Amarillo shut the door and turned to Angelica.

"What's going on?" she asked. "Are you ill, Mr. Breckinridge?"

"He may need hospital care after I get through with him," Amarillo muttered. "Take a look at this, Angelica.."

He picked up a large black case from the dresser, flipped the lid up, and handed it to her.

Puzzled, she stared down at the necklace, bracelet, and earring set that lay on the black velvet. The necklace was made up of three intricately worked, gold, vinelike tiers, interspersed with large, perfectly matched rubies. The earrings were a waterfall of vines and rubies. The bracelet, a wide gold cuff, was again set with the rubies. The stones were red—like the color in her dream.

"I don't understand," she said when she could.

"This looks like the setting for the Deverell rubies, but these are not the rubies." She sent the jeweler a bewildered glance. "The stones look like red glass."

"That's what I thought too," Amarillo said. "I was waiting for you to confirm it." He turned to Breckinridge. "Start explaining."

William Breckinridge sank into a chair and buried his face in his hands. "I never wanted to hurt her. I meant only to scare her."

"Why?"

Breckinridge lowered his hands to his lap but couldn't bring himself to meet Amarillo's hard gaze, so he stared unseeingly across the room. "I knew that at one time she had received a series of crank calls, and that she had been sequestered in her home. Most everyone who worked in the store on an executive level at that time knew. That's what I wanted to happen this time too."

"You wanted her sequestered in her home?"

"Yes. That way she would be forced to stay home and not attend the ball."

Angelica was hearing his words, but their meaning was eluding her. "What are you saying?" She glanced at Amarillo. "What is he saying?"

Amarillo's lips thinned as he continued watching Breckinridge. "He's saying that he's the one who made those strange calls to you, sent the note, slashed your dress, and today sent you the lovely clock that was intended to blow you to smithereens."

Her gaze flew back to Breckinridge. "My God!"

He looked at her then. "That's not entirely true, Miss DiFrenza. I mean, I did all those things, but you must know I regarded Elena DiFrenza as a queen. I would never have intentionally set out to harm you, her great-granddaughter, if there had been any other way."

"I caught him trying to leave SwanSea," Amarillo said. "We came back up here and I found the safe combination on the bed. At least he is conscientious when it comes to the jewelry owned by the store."

"I value my job, and I didn't mean to hurt you," he said again to Angelica. "In fact, I told the person who made the bomb for me to make it as light as possible. But I knew the red glass I'd put into the necklace to get it past the bankers would never fool you. So I had to keep you from the ball until I could get the real rubies back."

Angelica's legs gave out and she sank onto the bed.

"Tell us the whole story," Amarillo said.

Breckinridge nodded sullenly. "The last couple of years I've become heavily involved in investing as a sideline. I did well at it too. I seem to have a certain knack for it. I was really quite good at knowing how far to let a stock climb before I bailed out. But I was making money too slowly for my taste. Then recently I found a stock I thought was the one that would set me up for life. I cashed in everything I had, plus I borrowed money from people who weren't exactly on the up and up."

"That's wasn't very smart of you," Amarillo said.

"Oh, I wasn't worried. I knew I'd be able to pay them back. The stock climbed nicely, as I had predicted. But suddenly the company was found to be guilty of serious environmental hazards and the stock plummeted. I lost everything, plus there was the money I owed. They wanted it back. I had no option but to quickly recoup my losses. I knew I could do it if I could get back into the market, but I had to have money." His expression was defensive as he glanced at Angelica. "Then you asked me to oversee the cleaning and repair of the Deverell jewelry in the vault. Well, you can see, can't you, that it was a perfect opportunity? Those jewels were never worn. They were just sitting there, gathering dust. I decided to use them to help me. So I took the rubies out and reset the necklace with glass, knowing that should there be a random check by a bank official, he probably wouldn't know the difference. Not many people do."

Angelica looked down at the fake jewels. They were very good fakes, only the color was wrong. The color was red, *blood*red.

"You and Caitlin Deverell-DiFrenza were the only two people I was concerned about," he said, continuing, "and I had never seen either of you wear any of the jewelry from the vault. And the idea of a charity ball suddenly appearing on the social calendar certainly never entered my mind. At any rate, my aim was only to *borrow* the jewels. I wasn't *stealing* them."

Amarillo cut in. "What did you do with them?"

"I put them with the same people I had borrowed from before. They gave me fifty thousand dollars with the understanding that if I didn't pay them back the money within ninety days, the rubies would be theirs." His face took on a pained expression. "I *nearly* had the money together. I needed only another couple of weeks. If you had cooperated and stayed home, the rubies would have been back in their settings, I would have repaid my debt, and I would have had my money."

She barely heard him. She was mesmerized by the red glass stones. And everything was hazing over, *red*, like it had in her dream.

"Angelica?"

It was Amarillo's voice. And it was the last thing she heard before everything turned dark.

Ten

"Angelica." Amarillo stared down at her, the lines of his face deepened by worry. "Angelica honey, wake up."

Hearing him, she found his voice compelling. Her eyelids fluttered, then rose.

Relief hit him with such force, he felt weakened. "Don't move, sweetheart. I've called for the doctor."

She ran her tongue around her lips, moistening them. "Where am I?"

"I carried you back to your room. You're lying on your bed."

"Breckinridge?"

His tone took on an edge. "My men are watching him until the police arrive. You have nothing more to fear from him. I'm going to make it my personal goal to see that the United States justice system gives him everything he deserves. It's all over."

If only that were true, she thought. But the color red— She heard a knock on the door.

"That's probably the doctor," he said, rising from the bed and striding toward the door.

"Send him away."

He stopped halfway between the bed and the door. "No way, Angelica."

Her ballgown whispered and rustled as she struggled to sit up. "Send him away. I'm not up to being poked and prodded. There's nothing wrong with me that he can fix."

"It wouldn't hurt to let him look you over. Why are you being so stubborn?"

"Because I know what's wrong with me."

His face hardened. "Then you've got a choice, sweetheart. I'll send him away if as soon as I do you'll tell me what the hell is the matter."

"Amarillo—"

"Either that or the doctor is coming in."

Reluctantly she nodded and saw him open the door and say to someone she couldn't see, "I appreciate your coming, but she's much better and won't be needing you to look at her after all. I'm sorry if we've inconvenienced you."

"Not at all," she heard the doctor say. "Don't hesitate to call if you need me."

Amarillo nodded and closed the door again. "Okay, Angelica," he said, coming back to her side, "it's time you and I had a talk. You scared me to death by passing out like you did, and if you know what's wrong, I want you to tell me."

She glanced around the room. "Where is the Deverell jewelry?"

"On the table to your left."

She reached for the large case, and he came down on the bed so that he was facing her.

"Okay, Angelica, tell me what happened back in Breckinridge's room. Do you know why you passed out?"

It had been the red stones, she thought, gazing down at the top of the black velvet case she held in her hands. They had caused the red haze. The red haze just like in the dream. But that didn't make sense. It didn't, that is, unless she was, at last, certifiably crazy.

"Had you gone too long without eating?" he was saying. "What was it?"

"Amarillo, this is very hard for me to talk about."

Very gently he clasped her arms. "I've never pushed you, but I'm not going to let the matter drop this time. I'm not angry, but I want to know." He paused. "Why are you staring at the jewelry case? You're not worried about the real rubies, are you? I've already dispatched several of my men to an address I got from Breckinridge. We'll have them back before the night is over."

"That's good."

"Angelica, talk to me. *Now*. I love you, but I won't be shut out any longer. You talk to me now, or I'm calling the doctor back, and that's a promise."

She raised her gaze to his face. She couldn't doubt the love she saw there. Or the frustration, or the determination. "It's just that I don't know, Amarillo. The necklace . . . the red glass stones . . . I saw blood, and then they made this haze appear."

She was scaring him again, this time for an entirely different reason. But he couldn't let her see the fear he felt for her. He drew a slow, deep breath. "Okay, let's take one thing at a time. Where was the blood?"

"I—it was on the necklace." She shook her head. "No, that can't be."

"Lift the lid and look at the necklace."

"No—" She stopped herself in mid-objection. He was right. If she looked at the necklace again, maybe she could figure out what it was that was making her lose her mind. She had to be brave and look.

Slowly, carefully, she lifted the lid and gazed down at the three pieces of jewelry. Even with the fake stones in them, the intricate workmanship of the settings made each piece beautiful in its own way. But it was the necklace that drew her interest.

"Tell me what you see," Amarillo said, watching her closely.

Through the open French doors she heard the orchestra strike up downstairs. "Music," she said.

"You *see* music?"

"No, I hear music. There's a party." Her gaze was fixed intently on the necklace so she didn't see him frown. "And I see red . . . red."

"You mean the stones? You see the red stones?"

"No. I see blood. She's wearing blood around her neck."

Amarillo stilled. "Who, Angelica? Who's wearing blood around her neck?"

Tears sprang to her eyes and she tried to blink

them away. She looked up at Amarillo, but she couldn't see him. "What did you say?"

He was afraid to breathe, afraid to move, afraid he would do or say something wrong and send her over the edge. "It's okay, honey," he said very gently. "Everything's all right. You said there's music, and there's a party somewhere."

"Yes, downstairs. Mommy and Daddy are having a party. They can't hear me. I'm calling for them, but they can't hear me."

"And the blood, Angelica? Who's wearing blood around her neck?"

"Who?" She saw her then, as clearly as if she were in front of her. Her face was lined and heavily rouged. Her brown hair had silver running through it, and it was pulled back into a bun. Except strands of it were hanging down onto her face. And she wore a necklace of blood. And her eyes were open, staring blankly back at her.

Her hands flew to her mouth. "Oh, my God," she cried, "he killed her!" She began to sob uncontrollably, and Amarillo pulled her into his arms. "He killed her, he killed her!"

Once again he had no enemy to fight, so he did the only other thing he could. He held her tight and directed every bit of his love toward her. Each sob she gave tore directly into him, but still he held her. For his sake he wanted her to stop, and he never again wanted to hear such sad, pitiful, hurt sounds coming from her. But for her sake he knew it was important for her to release the hellish emotions that had been pent up in her for days now . . . perhaps for a *lot* longer.

She cried on and on. He still held her. He rocked her, he soothed her, he loved her.

He could hear the music from downstairs. Soon the ball would begin, he thought, vastly uninterested. There was only one important thing or person in the whole world and that was Angelica.

Finally the crying began to taper off.

"The dreams," she whispered after a while, "the awful dreams. They kept going after I woke up, and I didn't know what was happening. I thought I was losing my mind."

"Why didn't you tell me? Lord, why did you go through it alone?"

She drew back from him and wiped her hands across her tear-blotched face. He watched her and didn't try to pull her back to him. There couldn't be anything harder, he concluded, than letting her do things on her own.

"Because you deserved so much better than a woman doomed to insanity."

He groaned. "Angelica. Even if it had been true that you were having a breakdown of some sort, don't you think I would have wanted to help you? Be there for you? Love you?"

"But it's not true, *wasn't* true, thank heavens! Now I know what's been happening to me. I've been *remembering*, Amarillo."

"Remembering what?"

She paused, trying to find a way to put the newly remembered memories into words. "I was kidnapped, Amarillo. When I was very young. I'm not sure how young. Maybe two years old, maybe two and a half."

He started with surprise, then his brow knitted

with puzzlement. "Nico never mentioned a kidnapping to me. Nor did your father, or Elena. I would have thought at least one of them along the way would have made a reference to something as momentous as a kidnapping in the family."

She shrugged. "They didn't talk about it with me either. I don't know why they didn't. Maybe they were trying to spare me. It was probably very painful for them too. Maybe they thought it would be better if I didn't remember. You see, I *had* forgotten all about it."

His jaw tightened. "More than likely it was so traumatic for you that you developed a kind of selective amnesia about the event, even as young as you were, *especially* as young as you were. I saw it a time or two when I was with the police department. A person would just completely blank something out. It made things easier to deal with that way."

"Yes, but I've remembered everything now. The man came and took me from my bed in the nursery. I was wearing a nightgown, and my nanny made him wrap me in a blanket, but I think the blanket got lost somewhere after that."

"Your nanny knew him? She was in on it?"

"She knew him. I guess she was in love with him. I heard them talking a lot. She called him her 'golden-haired boy.' He was younger than she. Anyway, I don't know where he took me or how long he kept me there. But wherever we were, I think he must have kept me closed up in a closet."

Amarillo uttered an oath, but she went on. "There was a mattress on the floor, but it was always dark, I was always cold. And as the days went by—I have no concept of the time involved— I guess I naturally got dirty. I remember how furious he would get with me and how afraid I was. And how much I cried."

He reached for her hand. "I can't bear that you went through something like that. It just tears me apart."

She gazed at him and smiled tremulously. And looking at it, he thought it was the most beautiful smile he had ever seen.

"But I'm okay now. It's like I'm waking from a nightmare that's lasted for days. I can't tell you how relieved I am."

As beautiful as he thought her smile, he couldn't return it. She had already relived her hurt. He was only beginning to live it. "So I gather the dreams were you beginning to remember. But what I don't understand is what triggered the dreams? What made it all come back to you?"

"Breckinridge."

"What? He kidnapped you?"

"No, no. It was the wording he used both when he called me and sent the note. Now I know that he was just trying to get me to stay home, but inadvertently he chose words that triggered my memory. *Mind me or I'll make you mind me.* Those were the words the man kept saying to me over and over again. Then, *Be a good girl. She should stay home. She shouldn't go out.* Those were the words my nanny used to try to keep him from getting angry at me, but it was a feeble attempt. I suppose in her way she loved me, but she loved him more."

His grip tightened on her hand. "I hope she paid for what happened to you."

"Oh, she did. He killed her. I guess my dad finally satisfied his demands, because I remember one night the man jerked me out of the closet and then we were at a park or something. It was dark, and my nanny was there. He put me down on the grass. I remember how wet and cold it was and how loud he and nanny were arguing. She wanted to run away with him then and there. He wanted her to go back to the house and wait until a decent time had passed, and then join him. I don't think she trusted him, much as she loved him. In the end, I think he agreed to take her with him. She leaned down to kiss me good-bye and then she fell beside me. Looking back now, I realize what happened. He slipped a knife around her neck and tried to cut her throat, but she struggled. Apparently he managed to cut her, but not enough to kill her, because in the end he shot her. The explosion was so loud. By then I don't think I was crying anymore. All I remember is the droplets of blood lying on her neck like a necklace of rubies." She shivered. "My Lord, the horror she went through."

"What about the horror she put you through?" he exclaimed. "No child should ever have to go through that."

She nodded. "The explosions of the bomb brought the gunshot back to me; the red glass stones brought back the blood around her neck."

"What happened next?"

"I remember the police grabbed the man . . . some other policemen had found me. I remember being in a hospital. I remember my father visiting me there, but Mother never came. She was sick at the time, and now I realize she must have died while I was in the hospital."

"My Lord, Angelica! I knew your mother had died when you were young, but I didn't realize—"

"I didn't either," she whispered, amazed. "Not until now."

"No wonder your mind hid all this away from you! You were dealt two major traumas at the same time, and you were little more than a baby."

"I remember leaving the hospital and going to live at Elena's house. Daddy, Nico, and Elena were there, and they all practically smothered me with love and attention. I was happy, but I never saw Nanny or Mother again, and I've never connected any of this in my mind until now. Isn't that strange?"

"What's strange, not to mention remarkable, is that you went through all that and managed to come out of it normal."

She gave a light laugh, "Well, I wouldn't say normal exactly." She paused. "I think tomorrow we should go back to Boston. I want to see my father, and I want to call Nico too."

"If you'd like, we'll leave for Boston right now. That way you can see your father tonight."

She smiled, feeling such relief, love, and joy, she thought she would burst. "We have a ball to go to."

"To hell with the ball!"

"But this is a very special ball."

He started to make another objection, but then he stopped. For days now he had been tensed with fear and concern about her, so much so that he had almost missed what was right before his eyes: She was positively glowing with happiness. "A special ball? How could I have forgotten. It's in SwanSea's ballroom. The one that's warm and happy."

"That's right. And it will be the first time we've ever been in public together. It's perfect that it will be here in the ballroom."

He could feel himself relaxing, muscle by muscle. "There is that. And since we're going together, that means I won't have to watch you flirting with your date."

"And I won't have to watch some gorgeous blonde or redhead doing her best to enchant you."

He shook his head. "None of them ever enchanted me."

She wiped the last of her tears away, circled her arms around his neck, and used her most beguiling tone. "Then come to the ball with me, Mr. Smith, and let me enchant you."

"You've got yourself a date, Miss DiFrenza. But later."

A tiny frown touched her brow. "How much later?"

"However long it takes me to undress myself, undress you, make love to you, and then for the both of us to get dressed again."

"Oh."

His mouth was just about to claim hers when she stopped him. "There are two things I have to tell you."

"They had better be important."

She smiled at his growling tone; she was deliriously happy. "They are."

"Okay. What's the first?"

"The first is, I felt very strongly that I had to figure out the demons that were haunting my dreams *by myself;* I felt I was the only one who could do it. But I was wrong. In the end I remembered everything and I came out of the nightmare all right. But I never at any time did *anything* by myself. You were with me the whole time, reassuring me, loving me. Amarillo, I couldn't have done it without you."

He swallowed against the sudden tightness he felt in his throat. "And the second?"

"The second? The second is the most important. The second is this: I love you, Amarillo. I love you more than words can say."

"Then show me," he said with a low growl.

SwanSea was celebrating. All within its walls were safe and sound. Lights shone from every window, making the great house a beacon in the darkness. Music swelled and swirled, filling the ballroom, the house, and people's hearts, making everyone and everything laugh and be happy.

And when the lights on the fourth floor went out for a little while, the night and the house turned even more joyous with the celebration of living and loving.

THE EDITOR'S CORNER

As you look forward to the holiday season—the most romantic season of all—you can plan on enjoying some of the very best love stories of the year from LOVESWEPT. Our authors know that not all gifts come in boxes wrapped in pretty paper and tied with bows. In fact, the most special gifts are the gifts that come from the heart, and in each of the six LOVESWEPTs next month, characters are presented with unique gifts that transform their lives through love.

Whenever we publish an Iris Johansen love story, it's an event! In **AN UNEXPECTED SONG,** LOVESWEPT #438, Iris's hero, Jason Hayes, is mesmerized by the lovely voice of singer Daisy Justine and realizes instantly that she was born to sing his music. But Daisy has obligations that mean more to her than fame and fortune. She desperately wants the role he offers, but even more she wants to be touched, devoured by the tormented man who tangled his fingers in her hair. Jason bestows upon Daisy the gift of music from his soul, and in turn she vows to capture his heart and free him from the darkness where he's lived for so long. This hauntingly beautiful story is a true treat for all lovers of romance from one of the genre's premier authors.

In **SATURDAY MORNINGS,** LOVESWEPT #439, Peggy Webb deals with a different kind of gift, the gift of belonging. To all observers, heroine Margaret Leigh Jones is a proper, straitlaced librarian who seems content with her life—until she meets outrageous rogue Andrew McGill when she brings him her poodle to train. Then she wishes she knew how to flirt instead of how to blush! And Andrew's

(continued)

peaceful Saturday mornings are never the same after Margaret Leigh learns a shocking family secret that sends her out looking for trouble and for ways to hone her womanly wiles. All of Andrew's possessive, protective instincts rush to the fore as he falls head over heels for this crazy, vulnerable woman who tries just a bit too hard to be brazen. Through Andrew's love Margaret Leigh finally sees the error of her ways and finds the answer to the questions of who she really is and where she belongs—as Andrew's soul mate, sharing his Saturday mornings forever.

Wonderful storyteller Lori Copeland returns next month with another lighthearted romp, **'TIZ THE SEASON,** LOVESWEPT #440. Hero Cody Benderman has a tough job ahead of him in convincing Darby Piper that it's time for her to fall in love. The serious spitfire of an attorney won't budge an inch at first, when the undeniably tall, dark, and handsome construction foreman attempts to turn her orderly life into chaos by wrestling with her in the snow, tickling her breathless beside a crackling fire—and erecting a giant holiday display that has Darby's clients up in arms. But Darby gradually succumbs to Cody's charm, and she realizes he's given her a true gift of love—the gift of discovering the simple joys in life and taking the time to appreciate them. She knows she'll never stop loving or appreciating Cody!

LOVESWEPT #441 by Terry Lawrence is a sensuously charged story of **UNFINISHED PASSION.** Marcie Courville and Ray Crane meet again as jurors on the same case, but much has changed in the ten years since the ruggedly sexy construction worker had awakened the desire of the pretty, privi-
(continued)

leged young woman. In the intimate quarters of the jury room, each feels the sparks that still crackle between them, and each reacts differently. Ray knows he can still make Marcie burn with desire—and now he has so much more to offer her. Marcie knows she made the biggest mistake of her life when she broke Ray's heart all those years ago. But how can she erase the past? Through his love for her, Ray is able to give Marcie a precious gift—the gift of rectifying the past—and Marcie is able to restore the pride of the first man she ever loved, the only man she ever loved. Rest assured there's no unfinished passion between these two when the happy ending comes!

Gail Douglas makes a universal dream come true in **IT HAD TO BE YOU,** LOVESWEPT #442. Haven't you ever dreamed of falling in love aboard a luxury cruise ship? I can't think of a more romantic setting than the *QE2.* For Mike Harris it's love at first sight when he spots beautiful nymph Caitlin Grant on the dock. With her endless legs and sea-green eyes, Caitlin is his male fantasy come true—and he intends to make the most of their week together at sea. For Caitlin the gorgeous stranger in the Armani suit seems to be a perfect candidate for a shipboard romance. But how can she ever hope for more with a successful doctor who will never be able to understand her wanderer's spirit and the joy she derives from taking life as it comes? Caitlin believes she is following her heart's desire by traveling and experiencing life to the fullest—until her love for Mike makes her realize her true desire. He gives her restless heart the gift of a permanent home in his arms—and she promises to stay forever.

(continued)

Come along for the ride as psychologist Maya Stephens draws Wick McCall under her spell in **DEEPER AND DEEPER,** LOVESWEPT #443, by Jan Hudson. The sultry-eyed enchantress who conducts the no-smoking seminar has a voice that pours over Wick like warm honey, but the daredevil adventurer can't convince the teacher to date a younger man. Maya spends her days helping others overcome their problems, but she harbors secret terrors of her own. When Wick challenges her to surrender to the wildness beneath the cool facade she presents to the world, she does, reveling in his sizzling caresses and drowning in the depths of his tawny-gold eyes. For the first time in her life Maya is able to truly give of herself to another—not as a teacher to a student, but as a woman to a man, a lover to her partner—and she has Wick to thank for that. He's shown her it's possible to love and not lose, and to give everything she has and not feel empty inside, only fulfilled.

Enjoy next month's selection of LOVESWEPTs, while you contemplate what special gifts from the heart you'll present to those you love this season!

Sincerely,

Susann Brailey

Susann Brailey
Editor
LOVESWEPT
Bantam Books
666 Fifth Avenue
New York, NY 10103

FOREVER LOVESWEPT

SPECIAL KEEPSAKE EDITION OFFER

$12 95

VALUE

Here's your chance to receive a special hardcover Loveswept "Keepsake Edition" to keep close to your heart forever. Collect hearts (shown on next page) found in the back of Loveswepts #426-#449 (on sale from September 1990 through December 1990). Once you have collected a total of 15 hearts, fill out the coupon and selection form on the next page (no photocopies or hand drawn facsimiles will be accepted) and mail to: Loveswept Keepsake, P.O. Box 9014, Bohemia, NY 11716.

FOREVER LOVESWEPT
SPECIAL KEEPSAKE EDITION OFFER
SELECTION FORM

Choose from these special Loveswepts by your favorite authors. Please write a 1 next to your first choice, a 2 next to your second choice. Loveswept will honor your preference as inventory allows.

Loveswept ®

_____BAD FOR EACH OTHER   Billie Green

_____NOTORIOUS   Iris Johansen

_____WILD CHILD   Suzanne Forster

_____A WHOLE NEW LIGHT   Sandra Brown

_____HOT TOUCH   Deborah Smith

_____ONCE UPON A TIME...GOLDEN
      THREADS   Kay Hooper

Attached are 15 hearts and the selection form which indicates my choices for my special hardcover Loveswept "Keepsake Edition." Please mail my book to:

NAME:_____

ADDRESS:_____

CITY/STATE:_____ZIP:_____